My Magical
Story
Collection

Special thanks to
Anna Bowles,
Linda Chapman and
Karen King

ORCHARD BOOKS
338 Euston Road, London NW1 3BH
Orchard Books Australia
Level 17/207 Kent Street, Sydney, NSW 2000

Original editions of Enchanted Palace, Unicorn Valley, Cloud Island, Magic
Mountain and Glitter Beach published in 2012 by Orchard Books
This collection published in 2014 by Orchard Books

Text © Hothouse Fiction Limited 2012

Illustrations © Orchard Books 2014

A CIP catalogue record for this book is available
from the British Library.

ISBN 978 1 40833 016 6

1 3 5 7 9 10 8 6 4 2

Printed in China

Orchard Books is a division of Hachette Children's Books,
an Hachette UK company

www.hachette.co.uk

Series created by Hothouse Fiction

www.hothousefiction.com

My Magical Story Collection

ROSIE BANKS

ORCHARD

Contents

Welcome to the Secret Kingdom!

I'm Trixi, royal pixie and assistant to
King Merry.

Inside this book you'll find six brilliant
stories about a magical land called the
Secret Kingdom. Share the adventure with
Ellie, Jasmine and Summer as they try to find
all six of mean Queen Malice's nasty
thunderbolts, which are threatening
to ruin the fun in the kingdom.

Happy travels!

Love and kisses,

Trixi
x x x

Meet the Characters!

Ellie McDonald

When everyone else is baffled by a problem, it's often Ellie who finds a solution. She loves to paint and draw, and is always in the mood for a joke. Her favourite colours are green and purple.

Jasmine Smith

If there's a problem, Jasmine will march in and sort it out! She loves to perform and is the bravest of the three. Her favourite colours are pink and red.

Summer Hammond

If someone's upset, Summer will be the one to notice and help. She loves animals and reading, and her favourite colours are yellow and pink.

King Merry

is kind and clever but sometimes confused. He loves inventing thing and making his subjects happy. His favourite colour is royal purple.

Trixibelle (Trixi)

Trixi is always there to help King Merry – and Summer, Jasmine and Ellie too! She is brilliant at casting spells and her favourite colour is leaf green.

Queen Malice

is mean, mean, MEAN! She loves to make the people of the Secret Kingdom miserable and dreams of the day she will be their ruler. Her favourite colour is black.

Enchanted Palace

Enchanted Palace

Ellie Macdonald, Summer Hammond and
Jasmine Smith were the best of friends and
had been ever since they first started primary
school. They all lived in a pretty little village
called Honeydale.

Summer was quite shy and often had her head
buried in a book. Jasmine loved singing and

dancing and being
in the spotlight. Ellie
was a joker, and very
artistic. Together the
girls made quite a
team!

One day, they were
helping to clear up
after a school jumble sale
when Ellie stumbled across
a mysterious box. It was made
out of wood and thick with dust,
but under the grime she could tell the box
was beautiful. Its sides were carved with intricate
patterns and on the lid was a mirror, surrounded
by six green stones. Ellie wiped the lid with her
sleeve. As she held it, light swirled in the stones. It
looked almost…magical.

"How strange," Ellie murmured. "I'm sure this

wasn't here a minute ago."

Mrs Benson, the girls'
teacher, suggested that
they take the box home.

"Ooh, yes please!"
Summer smiled. "Let's
take it to my house and
try to get it open."

When the girls got to
Summer's house they raced
up to her bedroom and
placed the box on the rug. Rosa,
Summer's cat, came over to look too!
The three friends worked together, wiping away
the dust and dirt that covered the box. Now it
was clean, they could see that the sides were
covered in delicate carvings of fairies, unicorns
and other magical creatures. As the girls rubbed
the mirrored glass of the lid, Summer gasped.

"The mirror. It's…glowing! And look – there are words in it!"

With a shaky voice, Jasmine read out the words that had appeared:

"Ten digits make two,
Though two are too few.
But three lots of two,
On each jewel will do."

The girls looked at one another in amazement.

"It sounds like a riddle," said Jasmine thoughtfully. She stared at the words. "Well," she began, "riddles don't always mean what they seem to. You've got to look at things sideways. 'Ten digits make two'... The word 'digits' normally means numbers, but it can also mean fingers, right?"

Summer and Ellie nodded.

Jasmine sat up straighter. "So if ten digits refers to fingers and thumbs, that would make two…"

"Hands!" Ellie finished. "Ten digits makes two hands! 'But two are too few', so two hands aren't enough."

"'But three lots of two, on each jewel will do'," said Summer. "So three lots of two means three sets of hands."

Ellie's eyes gleamed. "That's it! The riddle is telling the three of us to put our hands on the green jewels!"

"Let's do it!" Jasmine said. She placed her hands on two of the glinting stones. Ellie and Summer lowered their palms to the jewels too.

The mirror

glowed brightly and light spilled out from between their fingers. The box burst open and a beam of glittering light streamed out, bouncing off the walls of Summer's bedroom. The girls watched in amazement as the beam hit her wardrobe and disappeared. Then the box shut again as if nothing had happened.

Suddenly, a voice came from the wardrobe.

"It's dark, so dark," wailed the voice.

"Please calm down, Your Majesty," a tinkly

girl's voice replied. "I'll find a way out."

Just then, the wardrobe door sprang open and something small and colourful zoomed out. Sparks flew everywhere as it whirled about the room. Then, silently and delicately, a tiny girl came to a stop above the bedside table. A tiny girl floating on a leaf!

The creature had messy blonde hair poking out from under a flower hat, big, blue eyes, pointy ears and a dazzling smile.

"She can't be real," Jasmine murmured, staring in wonder.

"Do you think she's a-a-a…" Summer could barely finish her sentence.

"A pixie?" The pretty creature smiled. "Yes! And of course I'm real," she said, doing a loop-the-loop on her leaf. "I'm Trixibelle – Trixi, for short – and I'm a royal pixie. Who are you?"

Ellie and Summer were too surprised to speak!

Jasmine stepped forward. "I'm Jasmine. And this is Ellie and Summer." She pointed to her friends.

"Jasmine, Ellie and Summer," Trixi repeated. "What lovely names!" The large, shiny ring on her finger twinkled with magic. She tapped it and a burst of sparkles shot out, forming their names in glittery writing in the air.

"Trixi! Where have you gone?" a voice called from inside the wardrobe. There was a crash and a small, rosy-cheeked man emerged from inside! He was dressed in a purple velvet robe and wore half-moon spectacles perched on the end of his

nose. He had a pointy beard, and a gleaming crown sat at an angle on his curly white hair.

Trixi gave a little curtsy. "This is King Merry, ruler of the Secret Kingdom," she said, zooming over to him on her leaf.

The girls looked at one another, then quickly curtsied as well.

"Pleased to meet you," Jasmine said in her most polite voice. "But what are you doing in Summer's bedroom?"

The king peered at them. But instead of answering Jasmine's question, he said, "Oh my! Are you humans? Trixi, what's going on?"

"I believe we are in the Other Realm, Sire," Trixi said, her face shining with excitement.

"Goodness me!" said King Merry. He stared at the girls. "You see, the Secret Kingdom and your world, which we call the 'Other Realm', exist side by side but our paths rarely cross. I don't know how we've come to be here."

Trixi spotted the box on the rug. "Look! There's the Magic Box, Your Majesty. Its power must have brought us here."

"This box belongs to you?" Summer asked, looking confused.

"Yes, it does," the king said with a smile.

"I invented it because I need a way to save my kingdom from Queen Malice. The next thing I knew, the box had disappeared, and we were in your wardrobe!"

"Who's Queen Malice?" Ellie asked. "And what is the Secret Kingdom?"

"Queen Malice is my sister." King Merry took off his crown and anxiously rubbed his forehead. "You see, the Secret Kingdom – my home – is a place of great beauty. A place where unicorns graze in emerald fields and mermaids live in aquamarine seas. But my sister, Malice, can't bear to see that beauty. She wants to make everything as dull and dreary as she is, and take all happiness from the land." King Merry stopped, his eyes welling up.

Trixi quickly tapped her ring and a white hanky appeared. King Merry blew his nose noisily before continuing.

"Ever since the people of the Secret Kingdom chose me as their ruler instead of her, she has tried to get revenge on us all by using her magic to make everyone miserable."

Trixi folded her arms angrily. "And now, on King Merry's thousandth birthday, Queen Malice has fired six horrible thunderbolts into the kingdom. Each one carries a powerful spell designed to cause a terrible problem. But we don't know where they've landed or what trouble they will create."

The king picked up the Magic Box and examined it closely. "I hoped

this box could help me, but instead I've
ended up in the Other Realm. It's baffling!" He
held the box out towards the girls. "You might
as well keep it. It can't help me if its magic has
gone all wonky."

Just then, another riddle appeared in the mirror
on top of the box. Summer read it aloud:

"Look no further than your nose,
Look no further than your toes!
When you gaze at me you'll see,
The answer's clear as one, two, three!"

Suddenly, Ellie gasped. "It's another riddle! I think the Magic Box is saying that the three of us can help you!" she cried.

The king peered at the girls over his spectacles. "The Secret Kingdom is in terrible trouble. Queen Malice will stop at nothing to spread unhappiness. It seems that you three girls may be our only hope! Will you help us?"

"We'd love to!" Ellie smiled.

"You try and stop us!" Jasmine cried.

"Can we go now?" Summer asked.

Suddenly, the mirror on the Magic Box glowed again and a third riddle appeared. Summer read it out loud:

"The thunderbolt is hidden close,
In the place the king loves most.
Magic made to stop the fun,
Must be found before day's done."

Trixi frowned. "Well, King Merry loves the Secret Kingdom more than anywhere else, but it's so big. We'll never find the thunderbolt."

"I think the riddle must mean somewhere special," Jasmine said. "Where's your favourite place in the Secret Kingdom, King Merry?"

"Oh, that's easy," the king replied. "It's the Wandering Waterfalls." He scratched his head. "Um, hang on…I do love the Topaz Downs. And the Mystic Meadows are wonderful during a pixie toadstool fight." The king shook his head. "Oh dear, I can't decide," he wailed. "There are so many places I love in the Secret Kingdom. I wish I was back in my palace, on my special

snuggly throne. I always think best there."

"Maybe that's because you're happiest there," Ellie said, her eyes lighting up. "Perhaps your palace is the place you love the most!"

"Why, I think you're right!" the king exclaimed happily.

Trixi bit her lip anxiously. "But King Merry's birthday party is being held at the palace today! If the first thunderbolt is hidden there, Queen Malice's spell will ruin everything! We must leave for the Secret Kingdom straight away."

Jasmine felt a buzz of excitement. "How are we

going to get there? Are we going to use magic?"

"Hang on, we can't just leave," Summer said, suddenly thinking of her mum and brothers downstairs. "What will we tell our parents?"

"Don't worry," said Trixi. "My magic combined with the power of the Magic Box will easily transport you to the Secret Kingdom. And while the three of you are there, time will stand still in your world – nobody will even notice that you're gone."

Ellie's eyes sparkled. "Then what are we waiting for?"

She held out the Magic Box to Trixi, who tapped the lid with her ring and chanted:

"The evil queen has trouble planned.
Brave helpers fly to save our land!"

Trixi's words appeared on the mirrored lid

and then soared towards the ceiling. The letters separated and descended like a cloud of sparkly butterflies. They began to whizz around the girls' heads until they formed a whirlwind.

"Place the Magic Box on the ground and hold

one another's hands," Trixi called.

The whirlwind now filled the whole room.
Jasmine squealed in delight as she felt her feet
leaving the ground. She looked round and saw
that Summer and Ellie had also been picked up

by the magical storm. She squeezed their hands encouragingly and her friends grinned back. The king had his hands over his eyes, and Trixi was hovering just above his shoulder.

"Secret Kingdom, here we come!" Jasmine cried.

Then, in a flash of light, they were gone!

With a gentle bump, Jasmine landed on something soft, white and feathery. "Wow!" she squealed. The girls

were each sitting on the back of a giant swan,
soaring through a bluebell-coloured sky!

"These are King Merry's royal swans," Trixi
told Summer. "They're taking us to his palace."

"They're so beautiful," Summer murmured,
stroking her swan's downy back.

Ellie, who didn't really like heights, peeked
over her swan's broad wing and gasped. Beneath
them was a beautiful island, shaped like a

crescent moon
and set in an
aquamarine
sea. The shore
of the island
glittered with
golden sand,
and in the
distance the
girls could see

emerald green hills and fields filled with little balls of light on shining stems.

As they descended through the fluffy white clouds, Jasmine felt her stomach flip-flop as she saw real mermaids sitting on shimmering rocks, combing their silvery hair! She could even hear their voices singing a hauntingly beautiful song.

"Welcome to the Secret Kingdom," Trixi said with a grin.

As they swooped down over the island, King Merry proudly pointed out areas of the kingdom as they passed: the pixie flying school in the Leafy Lands, Magic Mountain filled with sparkling snow-covered slopes and ice slides, and Unicorn Valley with its race course and enormous magical tree.

"Wow! Is that your palace, King Merry?" Jasmine asked, pointing to a fairytale castle nestled between two hills. A deep sapphire-blue

moat hugged the castle walls, and magic
seemed to glitter on the coral-pink bricks of
the palace, like hundreds and thousands on
cherry icing. The golden spires of the four palace
turrets were studded with rubies and shone in the
bright sunlight.

King Merry nodded and smiled. "Home sweet
home!"

The swans landed safely in front of the palace gates and the girls and King Merry climbed off their backs. The golden railings of the gates twisted upwards into the shape of a mighty oak. As the king pushed them open, the branches flowered with blossom and a fanfare sounded.

"The king is here!" Trixi announced as they walked into the beautiful courtyard.

A group of friendly green elf butlers, dressed in long black coats and white gloves, turned and bowed. Then they returned to hanging up bunting in the trees. As the girls looked closely, they saw that hundreds of glowing fireflies were clinging to the strings, making little lights!

"Oh my," the king breathed. "How handsome the twinkle-twinkle bunting looks. Trixi, my suggestion for the streamers has worked a treat!"

"I never doubted that your idea would work, Sire," Trixi said. She hovered above Ellie's shoulder. "It just needed a bit of pixie magic to help it along," she added in a whisper.

Ellie giggled.

As the king led everyone further into the courtyard, they passed a huge fountain

surrounded by a cloud of sweet-smelling bubbles.

"Hang on a minute," said Jasmine. "That's not water, is it?"

Trixi smiled. "No. It's lemonade!"

"A lemonade fountain!" Ellie cried, trying to catch one of the fragrant bubbles on her tongue. Summer and Jasmine laughed as they watched their friend.

Behind them came the clip-clop of hooves, and they turned to see a beautiful blue pony led by an elf butler, pulling a wagon loaded with brightly wrapped parcels.

"My birthday presents!" King Merry exclaimed excitedly.

But Summer wasn't interested in the gifts. She couldn't take her eyes off the pony and its aquamarine mane.

"He's gorgeous," she smiled.

"And he looks really friendly," Ellie added,

staring into the pony's warm brown eyes.

Smiling, Trixi tapped her pixie ring and a rosy-red apple appeared in each of the girls' palms. But just as they started feeding them to the pony, Jasmine felt a chill crawl up her neck. A dark shadow fell over the courtyard.

"Oh, no!" cried the king, pointing to the sky.

Floating over the palace was an enormous thundercloud. On top of the ugly grey cloud, the

girls could see a tall, thin woman with a spiky silver crown and a mess of frizzy black hair.

Trixi gasped. "Queen Malice is here!"

Jasmine, Ellie and Summer stared up at Queen Malice on her cloud, their hearts beating fast. Lightning crackled and thunder rumbled as the cloud stopped above King Merry's palace just long enough for a burst of rain to pour right onto his presents!

"Your birthday party will be ruined, brother!"

Queen Malice shouted at King Merry. She gave a mocking laugh, then the grey cloud sped off.

Suddenly, the presents in the wagon began to shake and little legs pushed through the wrapping paper. Then the gifts leaped from the cart and started running away!

"My presents!" King Merry wailed.

Trixi tapped her ring, but nothing happened to the presents. "My pixie magic isn't strong enough

to undo Queen Malice's spells!" she cried.

Ellie dived forward and caught an escaping gift. As soon as she did, the legs disappeared and the present sat innocently in her hands.

"Quick," Jasmine said, "catch the rest!"

Everyone ran after the fleeing gifts. Jasmine and Summer managed to herd three into a corner and pick them up. One ran straight through the legs of a surprised-looking elf butler, and Ellie, who was following it, couldn't stop in time and knocked him over! King Merry caught one by jumping on it, and then looked sadly at the present, which was now squashed flat.

"At least I can fix that," Trixi told him, tapping her ring and repairing it magically.

Eventually all the presents had been caught and changed back to normal.

"Queen Malice and her horrid Storm Sprite helpers are so mean," said King Merry. "She's

determined to ruin my birthday. I just know
that cursed thunderbolt of hers is hidden here
somewhere, ready to cause more trouble." The
king's eyes brimmed with tears. "This is going to
be the worst party ever – nobody will have fun!"

"Yes, they will," Ellie said, her eyes flashing.
"Because we're going to find the thunderbolt

and stop it from
doing any
harm!"

"That's
right,"
Summer
and Jasmine
chorused.

"And I'll
help too," Trixi
said, floating up
to the king's face and

drying his tears away.

"Thank you, girls," said King Merry, but his voice was still shaky.

"Bobbins!" Trixi called to one of the elf butlers.

The elf rushed over and bowed deeply.

"King Merry needs a cup of hot cocoa with extra marshmallows," Trixi explained. "And then he needs to change into his party clothes. His guests will be arriving in two hours!"

Bobbins lead the king away into the palace.

"Right." Trixi dusted off her hands. "Let's go and find that thunderbolt! We'll start in the gardens."

She stood up on her leaf and sped ahead, leading the girls out of the courtyard and into a maze with twisting paths that seemed to change every time they blinked. Summer, Ellie and Jasmine looked down every path but there was no sign of the thunderbolt anywhere.

Finally, the girls walked into a garden filled with trees made of candyfloss. Bunting hung from the trees and a group of brownies were busy putting lots of delicious-looking cakes onto a long table.

"These ones look amazing," Ellie said, pointing to a cluster of pink-frosted cupcakes.

"They're fairy cakes," Trixi explained.

"Oh, we have those at home," Jasmine said,

sounding a bit disappointed.

"Really?" Trixi said. "The magical kind? If you eat one, you'll be able to fly for five minutes!"

"Wow!" Jasmine exclaimed. "We definitely don't have fairy cakes like that in our world! Can we try them?"

Trixi nodded. "Just one bite, though, we don't want the magic lasting too long!"

Jasmine took a small bite of her cake. After a moment's hesitation, Summer did the same. Instantly, a pair of glittering wings sprang out on each of their backs. The girls zoomed through the

air, going higher and higher!

After a few minutes, the magic started to fade and Jasmine and Summer floated to the ground.

"Phew!" grinned Jasmine. "That was so much fun!"

Trixi and the girls continued to look around the palace grounds, searching for Queen Malice's thunderbolt, but there was still no trace of it. Eventually they reached an orchard where party games were being set up.

They could see a large barrel where seven dwarfs were practising bobbing for golden apples. Nearby, two tiny pixie girls were busy wrapping one of their friends in glittery pink paper.

"What are they doing?" Summer asked.

"They're getting ready to play Pass the Pixie, of course!" Trixi said. "It's a great honour to be chosen as the pixie in the parcel."

Ellie grinned as she spotted a

cheeky-looking imp drawing a unicorn on a wall. When the picture was complete the unicorn stamped its hooves and nodded its regal head.

"Let me guess," she smiled. "Pin the Tail on the Unicorn?"

Trixi nodded. "We'll also have Musical Thrones and Blind Brownie's Bluff. Then, of course, there's Musical Statues, but I've made the gnomes promise to change the guests back to normal straight after the game is finished this time."

Ellie and Jasmine laughed, but Summer's forehead creased with worry. "What are we going to do? The party starts soon, and we still haven't found the thunderbolt."

Suddenly, a burst of laughter whipped through the air.

"It's coming from the Outdoor Theatre, where the king's royal performers are putting on a show to begin the birthday celebrations," Trixi said, flying towards the arched entrance. "Come on, we need to find out what's happening!"

Ellie, Summer and Jasmine raced towards the archway and then stopped in horror. There, sticking in the ground, was a jagged black thunderbolt!

The girls stepped around the thunderbolt and through the gates. All around them, performers

were lying on the ground with tears streaming from their eyes.

"We've got the – hee-hee – the g-g-giggles," a leprechaun managed to squeak between screeches of laughter. "All of our scenery has been covered with black paint! Tee-hee-hee!"

Trixi looked angry. "Queen Malice," she hissed.

She tapped her ring and chanted a spell:

*"With this magic, hear my plea,
Stop laughing and act normally!"*

A shower of purple glitter spread through the air and settled on the performers. But they still couldn't stop laughing.

"Malice's magic is too powerful for me. We're going to have to cancel the performance." Trixi shook her head despairingly. "King Merry will be heartbroken."

"Wait," Jasmine said thoughtfully. " We can't let Queen Malice win. The four of us can put on the show! I'll make up a dance routine."

Ellie nodded. "If you can get me paint and brushes," she said, "I can easily paint some new scenery."

"I'll write a song to perform," Summer offered.

"That's a great idea!" Trixi cried. She whizzed
between the girls, helping out where she could,
and before long the scenery, dance and song
were all finished.

"But what about the poor performers?"
kind-hearted Summer asked. The actors,
stagehands and musicians were still lying on the
ground, giggling!

Trixi conjured up some floating stretchers,
which carried off the giggling performers.

From the wings at the edge of the stage, the girls and Trixi watched as the party guests took their seats. The girls had never seen an audience like it! There were dazzling unicorns, fairies with bright shimmering wings and adorable pixies, elves, dwarves and imps.

The audience let out a huge cheer as King Merry arrived, wearing his ceremonial robes, which were so long they almost tripped him up!

Trixi floated behind him, holding up the end of his robes like a wedding dress as he made his way to his seat, looking very excited.

Trixi tapped her ring and two spotlights burst into life. "It's show time!" she cried.

Jasmine took a deep breath, and marched out onto the stage. She felt braver when she saw Ellie's beautiful backdrops, with their paintings of mermaids, glittering golden beaches and snow-capped mountains.

"Welcome to King Merry's birthday party!"
Jasmine called. She threw her arms wide, just as
she'd seen performers do on TV. The audience
cheered in approval. Whispers rippled through
the crowd. "We have quite a show for you
tonight," she continued. "And we're not going
to let Queen Malice ruin the king's birthday,
are we?"

"NOOOOO!" the crowd roared.

Ellie and Summer joined Jasmine on the stage and Trixi conjured up microphones for them all. Trixi tapped her ring and lots of instruments floated up from the sides of the stage and began to play a cheerful melody. The three girls began to sing Summer's song. It was all about the Secret Kingdom and the places the king loved best.

The audience really enjoyed it and soon started singing along with the chorus:

"The Secret Kingdom is a magical place,
Even the moon has a smiley face.
The king's birthday will be a day of fun,
Malice's meanness will be undone."

Jasmine handed her microphone to Ellie and began her dance routine. The crowd clapped wildly in approval as she skipped across the stage.

Ellie gave Summer a big grin. "We've done it. We've stopped Queen Malice from ruining the party and—"

SPLAT!

Something hit the scenery. Six strange-looking creatures

with spiky hair, bat-like wings and ugly faces had swooped down into the open-air theatre, riding on mini thunderclouds. Their eyes were shining with mischief and their mouths were twisted into angry scowls. In their hands they held big fat raindrops, which they were hurling towards the stage!

"Trixi!" Summer hissed, beckoning to the pixie, who was hovering nearby. "Who are they?"

Trixi's face fell. "Those are Storm Sprites, Queen Malice's servants. And if we get hit by one of their misery drops, we'll be made as sad and mean as she is!"

From the stage, Ellie and Summer saw drops splashing into the audience, causing little rain clouds to spring up over everyone's heads. Soon everyone looked miserable.

The six Storm Sprites flew towards Jasmine, who was still dancing on stage.

"We're going to soak you!" one of the sprites said with a sneer. He hurled a misery drop at Jasmine, but she jumped out of the way.

"Oi, careful!" another sprite screeched. "You almost got me."

"That's it!" Jasmine said to herself. "If the drops hit the sprites, we can turn their magic back on them!"

"Quick, get beside me and wait for my shout," Jasmine called to Summer and Ellie. Six Storm

Sprites were whizzing towards her on their
rain clouds!

"One…two…three…DUCK!" Jasmine
shouted.

All three girls dropped to the ground just as all
the sprites released their misery drops. There was
a great SPLAT, and then a series of loud wails.
All six sprites had been hit! Little storm clouds

broke out over each sprite.

"Ugh!" one whined. "I'm all cold and wet!"

"Me too," said the sprite next to him, letting all his drops fall to the ground gloomily.

"Let's get out of here!" yelled another.

The sprites' rain clouds rose into the air and zoomed quickly out of sight.

"Yes!" Ellie cheered. "We did it!"

But Summer was staring at one of the misery drops left behind by the sprites. "I wonder if the misery drops can cure the performers' giggles?" she said to Trixi.

Trixi pointed at the drop. Her pixie ring gleamed as she chanted:

"Go to the performers, misery drop,
And make their silly laughing stop!"

The drop vanished, and there was a loud

cracking sound from outside the theatre.

Trixi darted to the theatre gates, and reappeared with a mass of ugly black splinters floating behind her. "They're from Queen Malice's thunderbolt," she explained. "When you girls stopped Queen Malice from ruining the show it broke her spell, and the thunderbolt shattered!"

Suddenly a storm cloud appeared overhead with Queen Malice on top, shaking her bony fist. "You human girls may have broken my first thunderbolt," she screeched, "but next time you won't be so lucky!" She threw

her head back and cackled with laughter as she zoomed away on her cloud.

"Don't worry," Summer said to Trixi, who was looking nervous. "We won't let her ruin the Secret Kingdom."

The others nodded.

"Oh, look," Summer smiled. "The performers – they've all stopped laughing."

Everyone turned to watch the royal performers walking out onto the stage. They were shaking their heads as if waking up from a bad dream.

In the audience, the rain clouds had disappeared and they all looked happy again.

"Now that the thunderbolt is broken, all of Queen Malice's mean magic is undone!" Trixi said happily.

"Let's do a grand finale to the show!" Jasmine said, turning to the audience. "I think we should all sing along for this one. Are you ready?"

The crowd cheered and everyone sang "Happy Birthday" to King Merry. His face broke into a smile and tears of joy rolled down his cheeks.

After the show had finished, King Merry came backstage to see Summer, Jasmine and Ellie. "The Magic Box was very wise indeed when it took us to you. Will you continue to be friends to the Secret Kingdom, and help stop my sister from causing more trouble?"

"Definitely," chorused the girls.

"We can't wait to come back!" Ellie grinned.

"You must promise to keep the Secret Kingdom a secret," said the king, looking serious.

"We promise," the girls vowed.

Suddenly three beautiful tiaras appeared in the air above the girls! Each one was surrounded by a sparkling glow. The girls gasped as the tiaras settled on top of their heads. They fitted perfectly!

King Merry smiled. "These tiaras will appear whenever you are here, and they will show everyone that you are Very Important Friends of the Secret Kingdom, on royal business."

Trixi also conjured up a magical map of the Secret Kingdom for the girls to keep.

"There are five more of Queen Malice's nasty thunderbolts somewhere in the kingdom, just waiting to cause trouble," she said. "The Magic Box will tell you when it has located one, and the map will help you find out where it is."

The girls nodded. "We'll be back whenever we're needed," Summer promised.

"Goodbye, girls," Trixi said, flying up to kiss each of them. "See you very soon!"

With a tap of her ring, Trixi conjured up a whirlwind that scooped the girls up into the air. Then, with a bright flash of light, they found themselves back in Summer's bedroom. Their amazing adventure felt like a dream.

"Did all that just happen, or was I having a strange dream?" Jasmine asked.

"It really happened," Summer breathed. "Look!" She held up the map of the kingdom.

"Where should we keep it?" Ellie asked.

As she spoke, the mirror on the Magic box glowed. Then, the box slowly opened, revealing six little wooden compartments, all of different sizes. Ellie gently placed the folded map into one of the spaces. It fitted perfectly!

"I wonder when the Magic Box will tell us that it's time for our next adventure," said Jasmine.

"I hope we don't have to wait too long," Summer smiled.

Ellie looked at the mirrored lid of the Magic Box and for a moment thought she saw King Merry's kind face beaming out at her.

"The Secret Kingdom needs us," she said softly. "I have a feeling we'll be back there very soon."

Unicorn Valley

Unicorn Valley

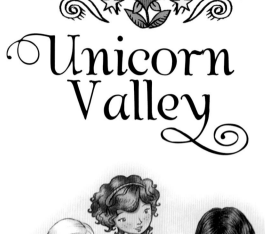

It was a rainy afternoon in Honeydale
and Ellie's best friends, Summer and Jasmine,
had come round to her house. The girls were
making biscuits.

Mrs Macdonald, Ellie's mum, came into the
kitchen. "Ooh, lovely," she said, admiring the

biscuits. "I'll put these in to bake, and call you when they are done. I'm sure they'll be delicious. And you've made such lovely shapes! Crowns and hearts and even fairies. What imaginations you all have."

The three friends exchanged a grin. Of course Ellie's mum thought they had good imaginations. She hadn't been to the Secret Kingdom, the magical land where only a few days ago the girls had met a real king wearing a real crown, seen fairies, and eaten magical fairy cakes at King Merry's birthday party!

"Let's go upstairs while the biscuits are baking," suggested Jasmine loudly. "And check on the Magic Box," she added quietly, as the girls headed up to Ellie's room.

The girls settled down on the window seat and looked at the Magic Box. It was just as beautiful as when they had first found it. Its wooden sides were delicately carved with images of magical creatures and its curved lid had a mirror surrounded by six glittering green stones.

"I'm so glad we found this at the school jumble sale," said Summer.

"The box knew we were the only ones who could help the Secret Kingdom!" smiled Jasmine.

The Secret Kingdom was an amazing place where lots of magical creatures lived – but it had a big problem. Ever since its subjects had chosen King Merry to rule instead of his nasty sister Queen Malice, she had been determined to make everyone in the kingdom as miserable as she was. She'd scattered six horrible thunderbolts around the land, and each of them contained a spell to cause lots of trouble.

"We've only found one of the thunderbolts she hid," said Ellie. "Trixibelle said there were six."

"I hope we see Trixi again soon." Summer smiled. "It was wonderful meeting a real pixie!"

"Look!" exclaimed Ellie, leaning over the box.

The mirror was starting to glimmer and shine. Words floated up from its shimmering depths.

"It's a riddle!" said Jasmine. She read the words

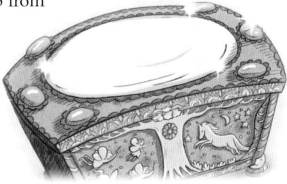

in the mirror out loud:

"The second thunderbolt is found
Where one-horned creatures
walk the ground.
Its wicked magic must be foiled
Before a special game is spoiled!"

Ellie crinkled her forehead thoughtfully. "Creatures with one horn," she said. "That makes me think of—"

"Unicorns!" Summer broke in, her eyes shining.

At that moment, the Magic Box began to glow even brighter. Slowly it opened, and a fountain of light shot up from the centre, lifting up a square of parchment. It was the magical map King Merry had given them after their last adventure! Jasmine unfolded it carefully. It showed the crescent moon-shaped island of the

Secret Kingdom. All three girls crowded round.

"There's King Merry's palace," Summer said, pointing to a tall pink building with four golden

turrets. The flags at the top of the turrets waved slightly, as if in a breeze.

Summer was looking around the rest of the map. "Flower Forest," she read. "Dolphin Bay."

"What's that?" asked Jasmine, pointing to a

wooded area surrounded by steep hills.

Ellie looked closer. "Unicorn Valley!" she exclaimed. "That must be where the next thunderbolt is!"

The friends pressed their palms onto the top of the box.

"The answer to the riddle is Unicorn Valley!" Ellie whispered.

For a moment the light coming from the box flashed so brightly they had to shut their eyes. Then it died away, and everything was still.

The girls looked around cautiously. Behind

them, the lid of Ellie's toy chest started to rattle!

"Don't worry," came a tinkly little voice from among the toys. "I'll be with you in a moment."

"Trixi!" the girls cried happily, recognising the voice of King Merry's royal pixie.

As they watched, the lid burst open with a shower of petals and Trixi shot out, riding on a leaf! She floated over to where the girls were standing. "It's lovely to see you again," she smiled, flying over to each of them in turn and kissing them on the nose.

"It's lovely to see you too!" said Ellie. After

their last adventure it had hardly seemed real that they had made friends with a pixie, but here she was, looking just the same – her clothes made out of leaves, messy blonde hair peeking out from under her flower hat.

Trixi's blue eyes twinkled as she smiled at them.

"We're looking forward to visiting the Secret Kingdom. We think the riddle says that Queen Malice's second thunderbolt is hidden in Unicorn Valley," said Summer.

"Oh, no!" exclaimed Trixi. "Unicorn Valley is one of the loveliest spots in the kingdom, just the sort of place Queen Malice would try to wreck!"

"Well, we won't let her," said Ellie firmly.

"Let's go and find the thunderbolt!" cried Jasmine.

Trixi gave the Magic Box a tap with her ring. Then she chanted:

"The evil Queen has trouble planned.
Brave helpers fly to save our land!"

Trixi's words appeared on the mirrored lid
before streaming up to the ceiling. They swirled
around in a glittering, flashing whirlwind.

The girls grabbed one another's hands. There
was a flash of light and then there, spread out
below them, were the rolling green fields of
Unicorn Valley. Fields that were getting closer
and closer!

"Aaarrgh!"
shrieked Ellie,
screwing
her eyes
shut. "We're
falling!"

"We're not
falling, we're

gliding!" called Jasmine from nearby.

Ellie realised that she was attached to a huge red leaf that was floating her safely down – like a parachute!

"I think I can see the whole of Unicorn Valley,"

called Summer, who was drifting underneath a huge yellow leaf. In the centre of the valley was an enormous tree that towered over all the others.

"That's the Great Apple Tree," said Trixi,
who was flying along beside them on her own
magical leaf. "And now it's time to land!" She
pointed to a corner of a field filled with flowers.
"That will work as a nice soft landing pad."

Flapping their arms and giggling, the girls
steered their leaves down to land on the bouncy
blue moss.

"Phew!" said Ellie. She felt something on her

head and realised
she was wearing
the beautiful tiara
King Merry had
given her at the
end of their last
adventure. She
turned around and
saw two white
unicorns galloping
gracefully towards

them. Their manes flowed in the wind and their
horns sparkled in the sunshine – one silver and
one gold. Ellie turned to look in wonder at
Summer and Jasmine. Their tiaras had appeared
magically on their heads too, and they were both
staring open-mouthed at the beautiful creatures.

The bigger unicorn had a wreath of plaited
leaves and berries resting on her mane. When she

reached the girls she gently touched the tip of her horn to each of their heads.

"That's a special greeting," Trixi whispered. "You should curtsy."

Hastily, Summer and Ellie picked up the edges of their skirts and curtsied clumsily. Jasmine, who was wearing jeans, had to hold out the edges of her top.

"Welcome to Unicorn Valley," said the unicorn in a kind but regal voice. "I am Silvertail, leader of the unicorns, and this is my daughter, Littlehorn."

The smaller unicorn whinnied. "I've never seen a human before," she said. She trotted round the girls, looking at them closely. "You haven't even got tails!" she said in disbelief.

Trixi cleared her throat. "Jasmine, Ellie and Summer are honoured guests of King Merry," she explained.

"We think that another thunderbolt may have landed here in Unicorn Valley," Ellie told her.

Silvertail whinnied anxiously. "My orchard-keepers did say that there was something strange near the Great Apple Tree."

"We must go and see what it is!" Jasmine cried.

"It'll be faster if you ride," Silvertail said. "I'll summon my strongest unicorns to carry you."

The three girls exchanged excited glances.

Silvertail whinnied softly. At once, three tall unicorns came galloping up. All of them had swirly, golden horns. Silvertail introduced them as Fleetfoot, Sleekmane and Greycoat.

The girls climbed onto the backs of the beautiful unicorns. With Trixi hovering beside them, the friends followed Silvertail across Unicorn Valley.

"Have the unicorns always lived here?" asked Ellie.

"No," Silvertail explained. "Unicorn Valley was founded by a unicorn called Snowmane many years ago. Back then, this whole area was covered with poisonous prickles. But then Snowmane touched a thorn bush with her horn and turned it into a lovely magic apple tree. The tree spread its beauty out across the land, and the poisonous plants disappeared."

"We look after the orchards and keep Unicorn Valley a magical place," Littlehorn neighed.

"Up ahead you can see Happyhooves Academy, our school," said Silvertail.

"Oh, the baby unicorns are so cute!" exclaimed Summer.

The group slowed down to admire the unicorn school. Riding on their strong unicorn friends, Ellie, Jasmine and Summer were soon close enough to see a teacher showing some

very young unicorns how to write their names.
Concentrating hard, they moved their horns
through the air and glittery, floating letters
appeared in front of them.

"Those little unicorns have silver horns, like
you," said Ellie to Littlehorn. "But all the big
unicorns have gold horns."

"Our horns stay silver until we're grown up,"
explained Littlehorn. "Then we take part in the
Golden Games and the elders turn our horns
golden. The games are this afternoon! The
winner of the Great Race gets to be one of the
king's royal messengers and carry urgent letters
around the kingdom. It's a huge honour!"

"I'm sure that's why the Magic Box has called
us now," Jasmine whispered to Ellie. "Queen
Malice's thunderbolt is going to wreck the
Golden Games!"

Soon the girls reached the orchards. "This

is the Royal Apple Orchard," Silvertail
explained, "where all the apples in the Secret
Kingdom grow."

Right in the centre of the orchard was the
enormous tree the girls had seen as they glided
into the kingdom. Its ancient branches stretched
out above them, heavy with gleaming apples.

"This is the Great
Apple Tree that
Snowmane
created," said
Silvertail.
"Without
it, Unicorn
Valley
would
turn back
into a wild
and dark place."

"It's amazing!" breathed Ellie.

Suddenly, there was a whinny of alarm from the other side of the tree. Trixi gave the girls a worried glance, and they all ran round to see what was the matter.

There, stuck deep in the earth between the roots of the Great Apple Tree, was a black shard that glistened horribly – Queen Malice's thunderbolt!

"Oh, no!" Silvertail neighed urgently. "If the

tree is hurt, its magic will disappear, and the whole valley will go back to being a wasteland!"

"I'll check that the fruit hasn't been damaged," Littlehorn said. With a wave of her horn an apple floated down from the top of the tree and landed on the ground in front of her.

As the friends watched, out burst a big, purple, black-spotted caterpillar!

"That's a slime caterpillar!" Trixi cried. "They usually live in the grounds of Queen Malice's horrible Thunder Castle. The more they eat, the bigger they get!"

The funny-looking creature nosed around in the warm air and stuck its tongue out at the girls before burrowing back out of sight.

"Yuck!" gasped Ellie, stepping backwards and knocking over a basketful of apples.

The fruit spilled out onto the ground, and more caterpillars fell out with it.

"Ugh, they're horrible!" said Jasmine, looking at one of the slimy creatures, which was chomping on an apple enthusiastically.

Summer watched a caterpillar as it swallowed a big chunk of apple and then burped loudly. "They're just hungry," she said, kindly.

"Summer you'd love any animal – no matter how disgusting it was!" Ellie teased her friend.

"Let's see if I can get rid of them," said Trixi, tapping her ring. She chanted:

"You greedy things aren't wanted here.
This spell will make you disappear!"

Nothing happened.

"Queen Malice's magic is too strong for me,"
Trixi sighed.

"What will we do if the caterpillars hurt the
tree?" Littlehorn asked. A sparkling teardrop
rolled from one of her eyes. Where it splashed
onto the grass, a tiny flower started to grow. "If
the valley turns back the way it was, we'll have
nowhere to live."

Silvertail looked at her daughter. "Why
don't you go and
practise for the race,
Littlehorn?" she
said kindly. "And
you girls could all
go and watch," she
suggested, turning
to Ellie, Summer
and Jasmine.
"Maybe you'll

be able to find more clues about what Queen Malice is up to, and work out how to stop her."

"I'll put a holding spell around the tree so that the caterpillars can't spread to the rest of the orchard," Trixi told them.

Littlehorn led the way out of the out of the apple orchards, towards the racetrack.

Summer noticed that Littlehorn was looking down at her hooves as she walked, with a worried expression on her face.

"Why don't you tell us about the Golden Games?" Summer asked to distract her.

The little unicorn smiled.

"Well, there's the Great Race, of course," she said. "And there are lots of other games and sports, and feats of unicorn magic."

"That sounds fun," smiled Summer as the girls reached the racetrack. It circled a playing field and a small hill, which was already crowded with unicorns watching the others practise.

"What game are they playing?" asked Summer, pointing to some unicorns who were using their horns to hit a bright red ball. Every time the ball hit the ground it sprouted little legs and tried to run away from the fielders.

"That's Run-Away Rounders," said Littlehorn proudly. She spotted some of her unicorn friends and headed off to join them for a practice race.

"Look, there's King Merry!" said Ellie, pointing excitedly. The little king looked smart in his royal robes, except that he had bits of paper sticking out of all his pockets, and ink stains on his cloak.

He was pacing up and down beside the track.

"He looks worried," said Trixi.

"Is he practising his welcome speech?" Summer whispered to Trixi.

"I think he must be," replied the pixie. "He's not very good at remembering his lines!"

The king stopped pacing and patted his pockets as if he was looking for something. Trixi flew forward and conjured a large spotted hanky, magicking his robes clean at the same time.

The king spotted the girls. "Hello!" he said cheerfully. "How nice to see you again. Are you here for the games?"

"Not quite," Ellie explained. "There's a thunderbolt in the roots of the Great Apple Tree."

"How terrible! Do you have a plan to get rid of it?" said the king, looking at them hopefully.

"Not yet," Ellie admitted. "But we're working on it."

"We won't let the unicorns down," Summer promised King Merry. But just as the words left her mouth, something dreadful happened!

Right in front of the racing unicorns, a cluster of long green weeds broke through the surface of the track. The nasty plants slithered out and tangled themselves in the legs of the running unicorns. Four of the runners tripped up and fell horn over hoof. Littlehorn only escaped by leaping high into the air as a stalk tried to grab her tail.

"It must be because of the Great Apple Tree!" Trixi cried. "With the caterpillars eating the fruit, the tree is getting weaker. And with its magic fading, the horrible weeds are

coming back to Unicorn Valley! Quick, head for the hill!"

Everyone started running up the hill. The girls and unicorns managed to scramble up quickly, but King Merry lagged behind. Trixi had to help push him up the slope. They had almost reached the girls when a weed curled around King Merry's foot and tripped him up.

Ellie dashed down to help him, but one of the vines wound around her waist and started pulling her down the hill.

"Get off our friend!" Jasmine shouted.

Summer grabbed Ellie's hands and Jasmine tugged hard at the clinging vine. With both of

them working
together the
vine finally
lost its grip
– and she,
Jasmine and
Summer fell over
in a big heap on
the ground.

The girls struggled back to the top of the hill, where Trixi, King Merry, Littlehorn and the other unicorns were standing.

"We'll have to cancel the games," frowned King Merry.

"Oh, no!" Summer cried. "If you do, Queen Malice will get her way and all the unicorns will be miserable. Littlehorn and the others won't be able to get their golden horns and you won't get a new messenger!"

"But what can we do?" Trixi cried anxiously. "Without the Great Apple Tree's magic, the valley will soon be completely ruined."

"Wait a minute," Ellie said. "At King Merry's birthday party, we broke Queen Malice's spell by making sure everyone had fun. So if she wants to ruin the Golden Games, then we have to make sure that they go ahead."

"But how?" Silvertail said. "We'll never clear

away all these weeds in time, and we can't have the Great Race without a racetrack."

Summer smiled. "I have an idea! We've got hungry caterpillars at the Great Apple Tree, and plants that won't stop growing at the racetrack…I think we should take the caterpillars to the Golden Games!"

"The caterpillars won't enjoy the games!" King Merry spluttered. "They're very lazy and they don't like sports."

Ellie smiled as she realised what her friend had in mind. "Not to take part in the games!" she laughed. "If we bring the greedy caterpillars here, they'll eat up all the weeds!"

Trixi danced excitedly around on her leaf. "I really think it might work, girls," she said. "I'll use my magic to take us back to the tree."

"I'll stay here, Trixi," King Merry announced. "Someone has to stay with the other unicorns and keep them calm."

"He doesn't like being magicked around," Trixi whispered to the girls. "It tangles up his beard and makes him dizzy!"

The girls giggled.

With Ellie, Summer, Jasmine and Littlehorn all holding on to one another, Trixi cast a spell:

"Help us get where we need to be
Under the Great Apple Tree!"

Ellie shut her eyes tightly, and when she opened them again they were all standing in the clearing by the tree.

"The caterpillars are much bigger now," Summer said.

"That's OK!" grinned Jasmine. She spotted a large apple cart nearby. "Aha!" she said. "That'll be perfect! If we load that cart full of the tastiest apples, the caterpillars are sure to jump in there too."

Summer thought for a moment longer. "I think we need a trail of food to lead them all the way to the cart."

"That's an excellent idea!" said Trixi, smiling.

The little pixie tapped her ring. It glowed, then something green unfurled from it and fell to the ground. It was a crisp, fresh cabbage leaf.

More leaves appeared from her ring, and Trixi arranged them in a line, leading from the Great Apple Tree into the cart.

One of the caterpillars raised its head, sniffing the air. Then it licked its lips hungrily, crawled forward and began to nibble at the leaf. It wasn't long before all the caterpillars were crawling up into the cart.

Once all the caterpillars were gathered up, Trixi tapped her ring once more and the whole group was transported back to the hill.

It was worse than they'd imagined. The racetrack was completely covered with horrible weeds, and King Merry was marooned at the top of the hill next to two sad-looking unicorns.

By now, the caterpillars were enormous!

"What if they're too full to eat the weeds?" Summer asked anxiously.

But when the greedy creatures spotted the moving weeds, they licked their lips and crawled towards them eagerly, making funny little gobbling sounds. They quickly

began to chomp their way through the mass of twisty green stalks.

"Our plan is working!" Trixi said, clapping her hands delightedly.

"Soon the racetrack will be clear!" said Jasmine as the girls moved the rest of the caterpillars off the carts. "Nothing's going to stop us now!"

Ellie gasped and grabbed her friend's arm. "Uh oh, something might," she said, pointing behind them. "Look over there!"

The girls turned to look. Two horrid-looking creatures were flying towards the racetrack on top of thunderclouds. Their spiky fingers were outstretched and their dark eyes gleamed nastily.

"Queen Malice's Storm Sprites!" cried Summer.

The ugly creatures zoomed closer on their thunderclouds.

"Give those caterpillars to us!" one shouted. "We're going to spread them around until Unicorn Valley becomes a wasteland, and there's nothing you can do about it!"

"We can't let the Storm Sprites take the caterpillars!" Summer cried.

Just then, Jasmine noticed something by the racetrack – a stand full of juicy-looking blue melons.

"Quick, help me grab some really big caterpillars," Jasmine said. "No time to explain – just trust me."

Ellie and Summer helped Jasmine carry three large, slimy caterpillars towards the melons.

"Phew!" puffed Ellie as she put
her heavy caterpillar
in place. "I get
it, Jasmine. The
caterpillars
will make
the ground
slippery, and
the Storm
Sprites will
fall over!"

"Brilliant idea,"
Trixi said as she flew overhead. "Those are
sugar-melons. They're so sweet and tasty the
caterpillars won't be able to resist them!"

Sure enough, as soon as the caterpillars spotted
the yummy-looking sugar-melons, they crawled
eagerly across the path to get to them, leaving
three super-slippery trails behind them.

"Okay, you win," Jasmine called to the sprites. "We'll give you the caterpillars. Here, take these ones."

The sprites laughed nastily, then hopped off their thunderclouds and flew down to the ground.

"Whoa!" shouted the first sprite as he landed. "It's slippery!"

His foot shot out from underneath him and hit

the other sprite on the ankle. The second sprite gave a wail, hopped on one leg, then stumbled across the track, waving his arms frantically.

The Storm Sprites had landed right in the slippery caterpillar goo!

First they slid into each other, then they tried to grab each other. Finally they both fell down in a tangled heap, squabbling.

The girls stood beside the road, giggling at the sight of Queen Malice's henchmen lying surrounded by squashed melons and slime.

The unicorns laughed too – all except Fleetfoot, Greycoat and Sleekmane, who were standing over the Storm Sprites, giving them very stern looks.

"You two are coming with us," Greycoat whinnied. "You can help us tidy up the orchard. That should keep you out of trouble until the Golden Games are over."

The unicorns marched the Storm Sprites off towards the orchard.

"There won't be any games unless the caterpillars have cleared the track," Jasmine said anxiously. But when she looked at the racecourse, there wasn't a weed to be seen! Lying sleepily on the grass, looking fatter than ever, were the slime caterpillars. The one closest to Jasmine was lying on his back, with his hundreds of feet up in the air, snoring loudly.

Suddenly Silvertail came racing up to them. "Queen Malice's thunderbolt has broken!" she told them excitedly. "The Great Apple Tree has already begun to heal itself!"

"We did it!" cried Jasmine.

"But what are we going to do with the

caterpillars?" asked Summer anxiously.

"We have to find somewhere else for them to live," said Trixi.

"Yes," Summer agreed. "We can't send the poor things back to Queen Malice."

But as they watched, the caterpillars started to wriggle. After a few moments, they had coated themselves in silk, which quickly

hardened into a solid cocoon.

"What's happening?" King Merry asked.

"I don't know," Silvertail said, nudging one of the cocoons with her horn. "But at least they won't need feeding for a while!"

Everyone helped move the cocoons carefully into the cart, where they'd be out of the way of the Golden Games.

"Now," said Silvertail with a big smile on her face. "We're ready for the Opening Ceremony. Summer, Ellie and Jasmine, you must stay and be our guests of honour."

Silvertail led the girls to the best spot on the hill, next to King Merry. Trixi magicked up floating cushions for them all, and they settled down as the young unicorns made the final preparations for the games.

Once everything was ready, King Merry's cushion floated up above the spectators and he nervously gave a little speech.

Then the parade began. Lots of little unicorns strutted smartly around the track. They all had different ribbons and flowers woven into their manes and tails.

The girls all cheered as Littlehorn cantered past proudly.

The unicorns lined up in front of the audience and sang the Secret Kingdom's national song:

"The Secret Kingdom is a wonderful land
From frosty mountain to glittery sand
Every unicorn, imp and gnome
Loves our beautiful magical home."

After they'd finished, everyone went quiet.

"Look!" Ellie cried, pointing at the sky.

All the little unicorns had raised their heads and pink and red sparkles shot from the tips of

their horns like fireworks! The sparkles swirled
and twisted into huge letters that twinkled
brightly in the evening sky.

"Thank you Summer,
Ellie and Jasmine
for breaking Queen
Malice's Spell!"

Summer read out
loud.

Then the letters
joined and changed,
coming together again
to spell out:

Let the Golden Games begin!

The girls oohed and aahed in wonder as they

saw lots of amazing events, but the high point of the games was the Great Race. Summer, Ellie and Jasmine held on to their cushions with excitement as Silvertail fired a burst of sparkles from her horn to start the race and the unicorns sped off.

"Come on, Littlehorn!" chanted the girls.

At first Littlehorn was in the lead! But a larger, red-dappled unicorn gradually overtook her.

Jasmine stood up and shouted encouragement while Ellie cheered and Summer crossed her fingers and pressed them against her cheeks.

"You can do it, Littlehorn!" Jasmine yelled at the top of her voice. Littlehorn lowered her horn determinedly and galloped as fast as she could. She drew level with the other unicorn — and then won by a head!

The girls watched proudly as the king crowned Littlehorn with a wreath of glitterberries and

officially named her his new royal messenger.

Finally, all the young unicorns climbed up to the top of the hill. The celebrations were nearly over and the girls knew it was almost time for them to go home. Only one last thing remained – to watch Littlehorn and the other young unicorns get their golden horns!

Silvertail whinnied and the unicorns all fell

silent. "This is when we perform the coming-of-age ceremony," she said, "and where we honour those who help us."

Littlehorn suddenly looked very serious. She and the other young unicorns gathered in a circle facing inwards and slowly lowered

their heads. As their horns touched, there was
a tinkling sound, and the air above the circle
started to glow. The girls gasped in wonder as
the little unicorns' horns slowly changed from a
sparkling silver to a glorious golden colour.

The noise died down as Silvertail moved into

the middle of the circle. She gave a long whinny, and all of the unicorns pointed their horns to one spot in the air. Bursts of sparkly magic streamed out of their horns, coming together to form a tiny silver unicorn horn! The horn floated over to the girls.

"This is a gift to thank you for saving Unicorn Valley from Queen Malice's meanness. Without you our beautiful home would have been destroyed. We will always be grateful," said Silvertail, bowing to the girls.

Summer realised all the unicorns were waiting for them to take the gift. She stepped forward nervously and carefully grasped the sparkling horn. It was no longer than her little finger and was covered with a beautiful spiral pattern, just like Littlehorn's.

Just then there was a gasp from the crowd. The caterpillar cocoons were moving and shaking.

All of a sudden one of them popped open and
a gorgeous butterfly flew up into the air. The
cocoons were hatching! Soon another butterfly
appeared, and then another, until the air was
filled with them, dancing and fluttering about on
their new wings.

Everyone admired the beautiful butterflies

as they flitted and
fluttered above,
oohing and aahing
at their dance in the
sky.

After a moment,
Silvertail hushed
the crowd. "Now,
Summer, listen

carefully."

Summer did so, wondering what was supposed
to happen.

Then she gasped. Amongst the flapping of their wings she could hear the butterflies calling out.

"Thank you!" they all cried. "We didn't mean to cause any trouble."

"I can understand the butterflies!" she said in amazement.

"The silver horn gives you the ability to talk to and understand animals," said Trixi, smiling.

Summer handed the horn to her friends so that they could hear the little voices.

Trixi tapped her ring and a sparkly spell in the shape of a butterfly appeared and flew away, leaving a glittery trail. "This will lead you to Flower Forest," she told the beautiful butterflies.

As the butterflies started to follow Trixi's spell to their new home, Silvertail turned to the girls solemnly. "You are now honorary members of our unicorn family. You are Summer Kindhoof, you are Ellie Flamemane and you are Jasmine

Braveheart," she said as she
gently touched each of the
girls in turn with her horn.
"Should you ever need
us, we will be there
to help you."

The girls looked
at one another in
amazement. "Thank you,"
Jasmine managed to say.

Smiling happily, the girls said goodbye to the
unicorns while Trixi conjured up the magic
whirlwind that would take them back home.

With a flash of light, they found themselves
settling softly onto Ellie's rug. The Magic Box
was sitting on the rug between them.

"I'm so glad we met the unicorns," said
Summer.

"But it's a shame that time doesn't pass while

we're in the Secret Kingdom," sighed Jasmine. "After all that, I'm hungrier than ever – and the biscuits still aren't ready!"

Ellie and Summer laughed.

Suddenly the box began to glow, and its lid slowly opened. Ellie gently placed the silver horn into one of the compartments inside. "I hope we can go back to the Secret Kingdom soon," she said.

"You can count on that, Flamemane," said Jasmine with a chuckle. "We still have to find four more of those nasty thunderbolts. I wonder where we'll go next!"

Cloud Island

Cloud Island

"I wish we didn't have any homework to do,"
sighed Ellie Macdonald as she walked home
from school with her best friends Jasmine and
Summer. "I've got to write a story for English
and I don't know where to start!"

"Let's all do our homework together at
my house," suggested Jasmine. "We can help
one another."

"Great idea," agreed Summer, linking arms

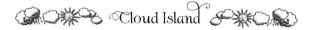

with Jasmine. "Even homework can be fun
when you do it with friends."

"I wouldn't go that far," grinned Ellie, her
green eyes twinkling as she took Jasmine's other
arm. "But it's better than doing it on your own."

Laughing, they all made their way to
Jasmine's house.

The three girls all lived in a village called
Honeyvale and went to the same school. They
had been best friends since they were little, and
they went around to one another's houses so
much that they all felt like home!

When they arrived, the girls put lemonade
and cookies on a tray and headed upstairs.

"Hey, you've got the Magic Box on
your dressing table!" exclaimed Ellie as
they spilled into Jasmine's bedroom, which
was beautifully decorated. The walls were
a gorgeous hot-pink colour, and red floaty

netting hung down over the bed.

"I didn't want to miss a message from the Secret Kingdom!" Jasmine said.

They all looked at the beautiful wooden box. It was covered with intricate carvings of fairies and unicorns and had a mirrored lid studded with six green stones.

The girls had found the Magic Box at a school jumble sale, when it had mysteriously appeared in front of them. It belonged to King Merry, ruler of the Secret Kingdom. The Secret Kingdom was a magical world that no one knew existed – except Jasmine, Summer and Ellie. It was a beautiful crescent moon-shaped island, where mermaids, unicorns, pixies and elves all lived happily together.

But the kingdom was in terrible trouble. Queen Malice, the king's horrible sister, was so angry that the people of the Secret Kingdom

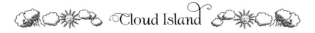
had chosen King Merry to be their leader
instead of her that she had sent six horrible
thunderbolts into the kingdom to cause all
kinds of trouble. Summer, Jasmine and Ellie
had already found two of the thunderbolts and
broken their nasty spells.

"I wish we could go on another magical
adventure now," sighed Ellie. She got her
English book out and started chewing on her

pencil. Just then, something caught her eye.
"Look!" she cried in delight. "The Magic Box is glowing!"

The girls all crowded around the box as words started to form in the magic mirror.

Summer read them out loud:

"A thunderbolt there will be found
Way up high above the ground.

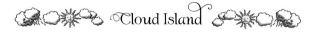

A white and fluffy floating land
Needs you all to lend a hand!"

"What does it mean?" Jasmine asked.

"Let's check the map," said Ellie. "We might be able to spot it."

As if it had heard them, the Magic Box opened up. Summer carefully took out the magical map and gently spread it out on the floor. The three girls sat round it, their heads touching as they peered at it. There were a few small islands moving magically on the map as the aquamarine sea bobbed up and down, but none of them looked white or fluffy.

"'Way up high above the ground…'" Jasmine muttered to herself. Then she glanced down at the map and laughed. "We need to look in the sky!" she laughed.

"Of course!" said Ellie with a grin. "What's white and fluffy and floats?"

"A cloud!" exclaimed Summer.

"And here's Cloud Island!" Ellie exclaimed, pointing to a puffy white cloud at the top of the map. "That must be it. Let's call Trixi!"

The girls put their hands on the Magic Box, pressing their fingers against the pretty green stones on its carved wooden lid.

"The answer is Cloud Island," Jasmine whispered.

Suddenly there was a flash of light followed by a squeal. Trixibelle had appeared, but the little pixie was trapped amongst the netting over Jasmine's bed!

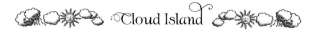

The girls quickly climbed up onto the bed to release Trixi from the gauze.

"There!" Ellie said, untangling the last bit.

"Phew! Thanks," the pretty little pixie exclaimed, flying over to kiss them all on the tips of their noses. "Have you worked out where the next thunderbolt is?"

"We think it's on Cloud Island," Summer said, reading the riddle out loud.

Trixi nodded. "There's no time to waste! We need to go right away."

The girls all looked excitedly at one another. They were off on a magical adventure – this time to an island in the sky!

As the girls watched, Trixi tapped the Magic Box with her ring and chanted a spell:

"The evil Queen has trouble planned.
Brave helpers fly to save our land."

Her words appeared on the mirrored lid and then soared towards the ceiling. A sparkling whirlwind picked the girls up, and moments later Ellie, Summer and Jasmine were dropped onto something springy. It was the softest landing!
Summer looked round in astonishment. It felt

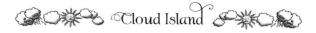

like she was on a huge bouncy bed, but all
she could see around her was white. She put
out her hand to touch the fluffy stuff, and
then grinned as she realised – she was standing
on a cloud! She could see the clouds laid out
below her like giant stepping stones. Beneath
that was the crescent moon-shaped island of the
Secret Kingdom!

Summer looked down as she heard a noise
from the cloud just below her. It was Jasmine,
bouncing up and down so excitedly that her
tiara fell off.

"Whoops!" laughed Jasmine, catching it. "We
mustn't lose these."

The beautiful tiaras magically appeared on
their heads every time they visited the Secret
Kingdom and showed everyone in the land that
Jasmine, Summer and Ellie were Very Important
Friends of King Merry!

Summer pressed her tiara firmly onto her head and then looked around for Ellie. She saw her lying flat on the cloud, holding onto the surface as tightly as she could!

"Oh, dear!" Summer cried. "Ellie's scared of heights! How do we get down to her?"

"We bounce, of course!" Jasmine replied, fearlessly leaping down to a nearby cloud, and then jumping straight down to Ellie's. "Wheeeeeee!"

Summer took a deep breath and followed her. She flew through the air and landed next to Ellie on the soft cloud.

Ellie groaned as the cloud shook. "Why do we always arrive so high up?"

"Don't worry!" said Trixi, flying down next to them. "These are trampoline clouds! If you do a little jump they'll spring you right over to the next cloud."

Summer helped Ellie stand up, and she and Jasmine both held onto their friend's hands as she started jumping about. Soon Ellie was

having so much fun she almost forgot how high up they were!

"Cloud Island is down there," Trixi said, pointing at a cloud far below.

Cloud Island was much bigger than the little trampoline clouds that led down to it.

The girls went from one trampoline cloud to another, passing surprised-looking birds on the way. The birds were flying from cloud to cloud with envelopes in their beaks.

"Those are messenger doves," Trixi explained. "They bring notes up to the clouds from the kingdom."

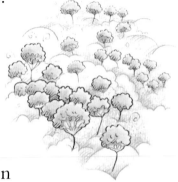

"Hey, look at those meadows!" called Jasmine. On top of the cloud were fields of pale yellow fluffy flowers.

"They're fluff flowers," Trixi told her. "The weather imps grow them to make clouds. But they also make a brilliant landing place," she added, flying into the flowers and scattering fluff everywhere!

The girls held hands as they leapt off the last trampoline cloud and landed on Cloud Island.

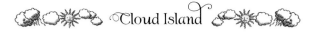

They lay in the fluff flower field until they'd
got their breath back. "This is much better
than homework!" Ellie giggled, putting fluff in
Jasmine's hair.

They walked to the edge of the field and
in front of them they could see a group of
funny little houses and factories and a tall
brick chimney with pretty white clouds puffing
out of it.

"The fluff flowers are cooked in the cloud
factory ovens until they're lighter than air,"

explained Trixi. "Then they come out of the chimney as clouds."

Ellie, Summer and Jasmine watched in wonder as a fluffy cloud squeezed out of the chimney and floated up into the sky.

"That's the most amazing thing I've ever seen!" gasped Jasmine.

Just then peals of laughter filled the air. The girls turned to see creatures flying out of the cloud factory on top of mini storm clouds. They had spiky hair, twiggy fingers and pointy faces.

"Oh, no!" Ellie cried. "Storm Sprites!"

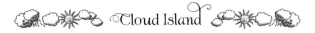

The girls shuddered as they watched the Storm Sprites zoom out of the cloud factory. The sprites were mean Queen Malice's helpers, and they made mischief wherever they went.

"Go away!" Ellie yelled as the sprites hovered overhead, laughing.

"Look, it's those smelly human girls," one of the sprites said, pointing a spiky finger at them.

With a screech of laughter the Storm Sprites dived towards the girls. Ellie ducked, but one of the sprites pushed Jasmine as he flew by and she landed on the cloud with a thud. Another sprite grabbed Summer's tiara and tried to pull it off her head.

"Leave her alone!" came a

shout from behind them. A girl wearing a fluffy dress ran over, waving her arms at the Storm Sprites. The sprite dropped Summer's tiara and flew up to join the others.

"See you soon!" he said, giggling nastily as they all flew away.

"Are you OK?" said the girl, as she helped Summer up. "Those Storm Sprites are so horrid. They're always here stealing our candyfloss."

"This is Lolo," Trixi told Ellie, Summer and Jasmine. "She's a weather imp. They live on cloud island and look after the Secret Kingdom's weather." She turned to Lolo. "This is Ellie, Summer and Jasmine," she continued, pointing to each girl in turn. "They're our human friends from the Other Realm."

"It's lovely to meet you," Lolo said. "Everyone has been talking about how you saved King Merry's birthday party and the Golden Games."

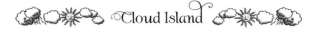

She looked at them, a concerned expression crossing her face. "But why are you here?"

"We think there might be a thunderbolt hidden on Cloud Island," said Jasmine.

Lolo's eyes filled up with tears.

"Don't worry," Summer reassured her. "We'll make sure Cloud Island is safe. But we need to find the thunderbolt."

Lolo lead the girls into the cloud factory to see if they could spot the thunderbolt, but there was no sign of it anywhere.

"At least we know what the Storm Sprites were up to," Lolo said, holding up an empty basket. "They've eaten all the candyfloss that was for everyone's lunch!"

The weather imps looked cross, but Lolo cheered them up. "We'll pick some more floss," she told them. "We need to check if the thunderbolt is in one of the meadows, anyway."

Lolo led the girls to the fluff flower and candyfloss meadows. They were delighted to see tiny white cloud bunnies hopping about the fields, chewing on the fluff flower leaves.

"They're so sweet!" Summer squealed as

she picked one up and gently stroked its soft fur. It looked just like a real rabbit, but it was much softer and fluffier, and it was as light as a feather. "I suppose even our Other Realm

bunnies have tails that look like clouds," she
said thoughtfully.

"Oooh, candyfloss!" Jasmine
said, looking at the meadow
of light pink sugar bushes
that stretched out in front
of them. "Yum!"

"Try some!" Lolo
laughed. "We need to
pick some for the cloud
factory imps' lunch,
anyway."

Jasmine reached down and
picked a handful of candyfloss, popping it in
her mouth. "Delicious!" she cried.

The girls got to work filling up baskets of
candyfloss for the cloud factory imps, munching
as they went. Then they took the baskets to the
cloud factory. There were also factories that

created raindrops, sunbeams, fog and snow!

Lolo led them round to some big circles on the ground. Ellie and the others rushed over and gasped – each one was a pool of brilliant, vibrant colour.

"These are the rainbow pools," Lolo explained. "We use them to create rainbows in the sky."

Ellie looked at the magical colours in wonder. "I wish my paints were as beautiful

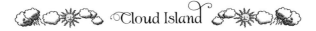

as these!" she breathed.

The girls wandered around, looking at the gorgeous pools. There were ruby reds and dazzling silver-blues, and all different shades of pink. They were all stunning — apart from one that was a purple colour, with funny grey bits in it.

"It's a shame this one's a bit dirty," Summer said.

Lolo rushed over to look. "There's something in here spoiling the colour!" she exclaimed. She

plunged her
arm into
the pool
and pulled
out a tiny
violet plug.
There was a
loud sucking

noise, and the colour started swirling round and round, disappearing down the drain.

As the colour drained away, the girls could see something black and jagged stuck in the bottom of the pool.

It was Queen Malice's thunderbolt!

"Don't worry," said Jasmine, putting her arm round Lolo. "We'll find a way to get rid of Queen Malice's evil thunderbolt."

But just as she spoke, a thick crack appeared in the cloud, right in front of the violet pool. Ellie, Summer and Jasmine watched in horror as the crack spread through the candyfloss fields, past the rainbow pools, all the way up to the sunbeam factory. "It's stretching right across the whole island!" Summer called.

Soon they could see right through it, down to the kingdom far below.

"The island's breaking in half!" Trixi shouted from above.

There was another big tremor, and the crack widened. To everyone's horror, the two sides of the island began drifting apart!

The girls looked around in alarm. On their side of the island were the fluff fields and the raindrop workshop, and on the other side, with Lolo and some of the other imps, were the cloud factory and the rainbow pools. Already the gap was too wide to jump across, and the other side of the island was moving further and further away from them.

"Don't worry," Trixi called. "I'll use my magic to put the island back together again."

She flew over the gap, tapped her ring and chanted:

"With this magic, my wish is plain,
Cloud Island become one again."

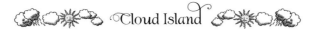

A shower of purple glitter shot out of her ring and shimmered through the air between the two halves of the island. But nothing happened.

"If Trixi's spell isn't working, this has got to be because of Queen Malice's horrid thunderbolt," Ellie said sadly.

The weather imps started running about frantically.

"What are we going to do?" one shouted. "If the fluff fields are on one cloud and the cloud factory is on another, we won't be able to make any new clouds!"

"And without clouds there won't be any rain, and all the flowers and plants in the kingdom will die!" another cried.

"We'll think of something," called Ellie.

"What can we do, though?" Jasmine whispered sadly.

Just then one of the messenger doves they had seen before flew down toward them with an envelope in its beak.

The girls opened the envelope. On it was a tiny moving image of King Merry!

The king looked worried, and messier than normal. His crown looked like it was about to fall off his white curly hair, and his half-moon glasses were lopsided on his nose.

"Is everything all right up there, Trixi?" the king asked, his voice sounding tiny.

"It's one of Queen Malice's thunderbolts, Sire." Trixi told him. "It's split Cloud Island in half!"

"Oh dear, oh dear." King Merry sounded very upset. "I'll come up there straight away and see what I can do to help. I can use the transporter that I've just invented."

Trixi frowned nervously. "But, Your Majesty—" she started saying. But it was too late. King Merry's face vanished from the paper before she had a chance to finish.

"Oh, no," she groaned. "I wish he'd let me magic him here! He invented a transporter last week and it keeps going wrong. Yesterday he tried to transport himself into his bath and he ended up in the sea!"

Suddenly there was a bright flash and King Merry appeared – right on the edge of

the cloud!

"Aaargh!" he cried, swinging his arms around to balance himself.

The girls ran towards him, but it was too late. With a cry of surprise, King Merry fell over the side!

"Don't worry – I'll save him!" Trixi called, tapping her ring.

A few moments later there was a very familiar voice from high above them. "Oh, gracious me!"

Everyone looked up to see King Merry floating overhead, hanging onto an enormous bunch of brightly coloured balloons! The king let go, landing on his bottom with a thud, making the cloud wobble.

"It's a cloudquake!" a scared imp shouted.

"Shhh, it's just King Merry," said another.

"Gosh, thank you Trixibelle," King Merry said. "I don't know what I'd do without you!"

Jasmine explained what had been going on.

"This is terrible!" King Merry declared. "We have to stop Malice!"

Summer twirled her long blonde pigtail thoughtfully. "In Unicorn Valley the thunderbolt shattered when we undid all the trouble it had caused."

"So if we can put the island back together again it might break Queen Malice's spell," Jasmine suggested.

"That's it!" Summer cried. "We could glue it back together with new clouds from the factory! Lolo!" she called to the imp on the other cloud. "Can we stick the island back together with new clouds?"

Lolo shook her head sadly. "We can't make clouds quickly enough to repair a crack this big," she replied.

"We need to stick it together with something

else, just while the cloud's being made," Jasmine sighed.

"Maybe we can glue it back together with candyfloss!" said Ellie, her eyes gleaming.

"That could work," said Trixi thoughtfully. "But I don't know how we can bring the other half of the island here so we can stick it together."

"There must be some way we can pull the broken part back over here…"muttered Jasmine.

Ellie looked around Cloud Island for inspiration. Then her eyes rested on the little dove, still perched next to Summer.

"The messenger doves!" she cried. "They could flap their wings and blow the broken half back over to us!" She sighed. "If only we could talk to them and explain what we wanted them to do."

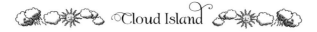

With a shimmer, the Magic Box appeared in front of them.

"Of course!" Summer cried. "We can use the unicorn horn to talk to them!" She grinned, as she picked up the magical horn the unicorns had given them. When the girls held it they had the ability to talk to all the  animals in the Secret Kingdom! Summer turned to the white dove. "Please can you help us?" she said.

"Me?" Summer heard the dove coo in a surprised voice. "Of course, if I can. What's wrong?"

"A cloudquake has split Cloud Island in two,"

she told the bird. "Could you gather all of your friends and beat your wings at the same time to make some wind? It might be strong enough to blow the broken part back over to us."

"We're going to need a lot of wing power," replied the bird, flapping into the air. "I'll gather the flock."

"Let's tell Lolo about our plan!" Jasmine said,

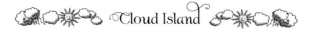
excitedly. They hurried to the edge. The other half of the island was further away than ever, but Lolo was still close enough to hear as the girls shouted the plan over.

"Great!" she called back. "We'll start making as much cloud as we can and collect the floss."

"And I'll supervise over here!" yelled King Merry. "I love candyfloss... I mean, I

love gathering candyfloss!"

Trixi smiled. "He'll probably eat more than he collects!" she whispered with a giggle.

The girls, King Merry and the weather imps all bustled around the candyfloss meadow collecting armfuls of the sticky pink stuff. Then everyone knelt down and started to spread the floss on the edges of the crack. Soon their side of the edge was covered in the sticky stuff.

"We've finished just in time!" gasped Jasmine as a big flock of doves flew towards them.

The birds circled the broken half of the island and started beating their wings. Their wings made a strong wind, and the broken section gradually started to move.

"It's working!" shouted Ellie, jumping up and down with excitement.

The weather imps gathered on both edges, cheering loudly.

"Well done!" they called to the doves. "Keep going!"

But just as the two halves of the island were almost touching, four spiky-haired

creatures zoomed into the gap.

"Aha!" one shrieked. "The Storm Sprites are here to spoil your day!"

The Storm Sprites whooped and cackled and started to beat their powerful wings. The blast of wind almost blew the girls off their feet.

"They're pushing the island apart again!" cried Ellie.

"We've got to do something," said Jasmine, looking at the widening gulf of blue sky between the two halves of the island.

"I've got an idea," said Summer. She rushed over to the raindrop workshop and scooped up some of the candyfloss from the heap. "Yum!" she cried loudly. "This candyfloss is delicious! Do you want some, Ellie?"

"I don't think we have time…" Ellie stopped as Summer nodded her head over to the Storm Sprites, who were looking hungrily at

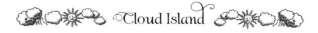

the big pile of candyfloss.

"Oh, thanks, Summer!" she said loudly, taking a bite. "Mmmmm, lovely candyfloss. Jasmine, come and have some!"

The Storm Sprites were licking their lips now.

"They've got candyfloss," one whispered longingly. "Queen Malice never lets us eat candyfloss!"

"Good idea, Summer!" Ellie whispered.

"Food always distracts my brothers, too!"
Summer giggled.

"We'll just leave this big pile of delicious
candyfloss here while we go over
there," Jasmine said loudly, winking at Ellie
and Summer.

The three girls walked away,
and Ellie peeked over
her shoulder. The sprites
had all rushed over to
the candyfloss and were
greedily stuffing it into
their mouths.

While they were busy
eating, Summer spoke to the doves. "Quick!
Start blowing the island back together again!"
she cooed.

The doves circled the broken piece and
beat their wings with all their might. Slowly

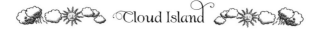

it started to drift back towards the rest of
Cloud Island.

"They've nearly done it," whispered Jasmine.

But then one of the Storm Sprites turned
round. "We've been tricked!" he screeched.
"We'll be in big trouble if those girls beat us
again. The queen will lock us in the dungeons!"

The sprites rushed towards the gap, but Ellie,
Summer and Jasmine grabbed handfuls of
candyfloss and started throwing it at the sprites!

"Take that!" Ellie yelled, throwing a sticky
missile at one of the sprites. The floss hit him
with a squelchy thud.

The naughty sprites tried to pull the
candyfloss off one another, but then their hands
started sticking together!

The girls, King Merry, Trixi and the weather
imps all giggled at the sticky sprites. They
looked so funny covered in pink goo!

The sprites tried to make some wind to blow the pieces of the island apart, but their wings were so covered with candyfloss that they stuck together and wouldn't flap.

"Retreat! Retreat!" shouted the leader.

The Storm Sprites jumped on their clouds and zoomed down to the kingdom below.

"We've done it!" Ellie shouted. The three girls hugged each other. Now that the Storm Sprites were out of the way, the doves were able to blow the broken pieces of the island together. With a jolt, Cloud Island was finally joined up again, the sticky candyfloss holding it fast.

"Hooray!" the imps all shouted, clapping.

Ellie and Jasmine waved. "Thank you!" they called to the doves.

"Our pleasure," cooed the dove. Then he waved his wing and flew off with the others.

Lolo and the other imps rushed over.

"Now to mend this crack once and for all," Lolo said firmly. "Quick – start making as much cloud as you can," she told the other weather imps.

The imps rushed about, busily collecting fluff flowers and feeding them into the cloud factory.

Summer had an armful of fluff flowers and was bending over to pick more when a dark

shadow fell across the ground. She looked up
and gasped.

There was a thundercloud heading right
for them…and on top of it stood a tall, thin
woman with wild, frizzy hair. She was wearing
a black cloak and a spiky silver crown.

"It's Queen Malice!" Summer cried.

Queen Malice's cloud stopped right over the line of candyfloss and a shower of rain began to gush from underneath it.

"Oh, no!" gasped Summer. "She's trying to wash the candyfloss away! It needs to be

sticky, instead of soggy!"

"You girls won't destroy this thunderbolt,"
Queen Malice called down from her cloud. "I
will break Cloud Island apart and the Secret
Kingdom will turn into a dry desert. My useless
brother won't know what to do and then you'll
all be begging me to rule!"

Jasmine looked around desperately. "We
need to stop the water from falling on the

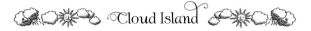

candyfloss," she told the others. "Trixi, can you magic something up to catch it? An umbrella, or a blanket or something?"

Trixi tapped her ring and a stripy bucket floated down from the sky.

Jasmine jumped up to catch it, and rushed to put it under the raincloud. Soon there were hundreds of buckets of all sizes and colours keeping the candyfloss nice and dry. Raindrops plopped noisily into them.

"We need somewhere to empty them out," said Summer.

Ellie was standing closest to the edge of Cloud Island. She peered over and saw a pretty forest of tall flowers below. The Storm Sprites were sitting in the centre of one of the gigantic flowers, picking candyfloss off their wings and squabbling noisily.

"Those giant flowers look like they could do

with a drink," Ellie said.

"And the Storm Sprites could do with a
bath!" Summer giggled.

As the buckets filled up, Summer, Ellie,
Jasmine, King Merry and all the weather imps
started emptying them over the side.

Jasmine peered up at Queen Malice's cloud and noticed something – it was moving upwards. "Look!" she called. As the girls watched, the cloud rose higher and higher.

"Stop moving me!' shrieked Queen Malice.

"It's not us!" Jasmine yelled up to her. "Your cloud's much lighter without all that rain, so it's floating away!"

As the thundercloud drifted higher, the rain slowed to a drizzle and then stopped.

"Nooooo!" Queen

Malice wailed from above.

"The new cloud's ready," called an imp from the cloud factory.

"Quick, empty the rest of the buckets," Lolo called. The girls rushed to pour the water onto the flowers below. Jasmine was going so fast that she accidently let go of the bucket, and it fell over the side as well.

"Oops!" she said peering over the edge. The bucket had landed upside down on the head of one of the Storm Sprites!

"Who turned out the lights?" he squawked, sticking his arms out and accidently pushing another sprite off the flower and into a puddle of mud on the ground.

"Nice hat," Ellie called down to him.

With the rain emptied, the girls went to help the imps, who were bringing basket after basket of new cloud over to the crack.

Everyone helped smooth the
cloud over the gap. Soon
you couldn't even see
where the join was.

Suddenly there was a
loud cracking sound.

Ellie looked over at the violet pool just
in time to see the ugly black thunderbolt
shattering into hundreds of pieces.

"We've broken the spell!" she said delightedly.

"Nooooo!" Queen Malice yelled from far
above. "My beautiful thunderbolt!"

Her cloud was so high they could hardly see
it any more, but they could still hear the mean
queen's voice as she shouted nastily, "There
are still three more of my thunderbolts in the
kingdom and you'll never find them! I will not
be defeated…"

Queen Malice's voice finally faded into the

distance, and she and her cloud were gone.

Lolo came over, smiling happily. "Thanks to you, Cloud Island is back together again!"

"Hooray!" the girls all cheered.

"I guess that means it's time for us to go home," Ellie sighed.

"Oh, but you'll come and visit us again, won't you?" said Lolo as all the weather imps

gathered around to say goodbye. "We could never have fixed Cloud Island without you."

"We'd love to," said Jasmine.

Summer said goodbye to the friendly little cloud bunny. She picked him

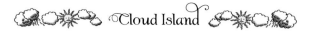

up and stroked his tiny soft ears, trying not to feel sad.

"We wanted to give you a thank-you gift," Lolo smiled. She held up a beautiful, sparkling jewel. "This is a weather crystal," she said, handing it to Jasmine. "It gives you the power to change the weather, just for a little while."

Jasmine took the gleaming crystal.

"Concentrate on the weather you want," Lolo told her.

Jasmine gazed at the crystal and thought hard. Suddenly glorious sunshine filled the sky!

"Oh, thank you!" Jasmine said, holding up the crystal for Summer and Ellie to see.

"It's so beautiful!" said Summer, dancing in and out of the sunbeams.

"Ready to go, girls?" asked Trixi.

"Ready," they all said.

Trixi tapped her ring. A whirlwind started to form, growing bigger and bigger until in a flash they were back in Jasmine's bedroom again.

Ellie looked at the clock, but no time had passed. Somehow, time always stood still when they went to the Secret Kingdom!

The girls put the magical gifts away. Summer placed the horn in one of the compartments, next to the map. Jasmine held up the weather crystal and they all looked at it one more time before she carefully placed it in the Magic Box.

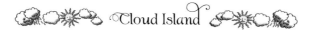

"I guess we'd better get started with that homework," Ellie sighed.

"I know what you can write your story about," smiled Summer. "Cloud Island and the weather imps!"

Ellie grinned and pulled open her book. She couldn't wait to describe all the magical things she'd seen on Cloud Island – and imagine what they'd do on their next visit to the Secret Kingdom!

Mermaid Reef

Mermaid Reef

"I'm starving!" cried Jasmine Smith as she joined her friends Ellie Macdonald and Summer Hammond in the busy school canteen.

As she pulled her lunchbox out of her bag, Jasmine suddenly noticed that deep at the bottom of her bag there was a familiar sparkly glow…"The Magic Box!" she whispered.

"What?" Ellie gasped, almost knocking her

drink over in excitement.
The Magic Box had never
sent them a message at
school before!

The beautiful box had
been created by King
Merry, the ruler of the
Secret Kingdom.

The Secret Kingdom was a magical land full
of unicorns, mermaids, pixies and elves – but it
had a terrible problem. When King Merry had
been chosen by his subjects to rule the kingdom
instead of his nasty sister, Queen Malice, the
horrid queen had been so annoyed that she had
thrown six enchanted thunderbolts into the most
wonderful places in the land to ruin them and
make everyone as miserable as she was!

King Merry had sent the Magic Box to find
the only people who could help save the

kingdom – Jasmine, Summer and Ellie! The girls had already helped the king and his pixie assistant Trixibelle destroy three of the horrible thunderbolts. Now it looked like they were needed to find another one.

The three friends rushed into the toilets. Time stood still while they were in the Secret Kingdom, so no one would realise they were gone!

They closed the door of a cubicle and crowded around the box.

"The riddle's appearing!" Summer whispered.

The girls all watched eagerly as words started to form in the mirrored lid:

"Another thunderbolt is near,
Way down deep in water clear.
Look on the bed that's in the sea,
Where more than fish swim happily!"

Ellie slowly read out the rhyme. 'What do you think that means?"

Jasmine frowned. "Well, the bottom of the sea is called the seabed…"

Suddenly the lid of the Magic Box opened, revealing the six little wooden compartments inside. Three of the spaces were already filled with the wonderful gifts they'd been given by the people of the Secret Kingdom. There was a magical moving map that showed them all the places in the kingdom, a tiny silver unicorn horn

that let them talk to animals and a shimmering crystal that had the power to change the weather. Jasmine carefully took the map out. "Look," she said, pointing to the aquamarine sea. Waves were gently spilling onto the shore, colourful fish were playing in the water and a beautiful girl was sitting on a rock, combing her hair.

As Ellie, Summer and Jasmine watched, the girl dived off the rock into the sparkling water. Jasmine gasped as she saw that, instead of legs, she had a glittering tail!

"She's a mermaid!" Jasmine cried to the others, who nodded excitedly.

They watched the mermaid as she swam down to where an underwater town was marked. Ellie held the map up and looked at the place name. "'Mermaid Reef'," she read.

The three friends quickly placed their fingertips on the jewels on the Magic Box.

Summer said the answer to the riddle out loud: "Mermaid Reef."

A glittering light beamed out from the mirror. Then there was a golden flash and Trixi appeared, twirling in midair like a ballerina. Her blue eyes twinkled happily as she balanced on her leaf.

"Hi, Trixi," Ellie cried in delight as the pixie hovered gracefully just in front of the girls.

"Hello," Trixi said, smiling. "It's great to see you!" Then the little pixie's face took on a worried expression. "Do you know where Queen Malice's next thunderbolt is?"

"We think it's in Mermaid Reef," Ellie told her.

"Then we must go at once!" Trixi exclaimed. "The mermaids will need our help."

"We are going to meet mermaids!" Summer squealed as she jumped up and down with excitement.

Trixi giggled, then tapped her ring and chanted:

*"The evil queen has trouble planned.
Brave helpers fly to save our land!"*

As she spoke, a magical whirlwind surrounded the girls. Seconds later, they found themselves on a smooth green rock in the

middle of the sea. They were delighted to be wearing their sparkly tiaras once again, although they were still in their school uniforms! The girls watched as the water started to churn in front of them and a huge green head appeared out of the water. Summer broke out in a grin.

"Look!" she cried, pointing at the animal's face. "We're not standing on a rock, we're standing on the back of a giant sea turtle!"

"A lift from a turtle is the only way to get to Mermaid Reef!" Trixi cried. She tapped her ring and a stream of purple bubbles shot out of it, showering the girls with glitter.

"Hold on tight!" Trixi called.

"Trixi, wait!" Jasmine cried. "We can't breathe underwater!"

But it was too late. The huge turtle dived deep into the sea…

Jasmine quickly clamped her mouth shut as the water covered her face.

Trixi gave a tinkly laugh. "Don't worry!" she explained. "The bubble dust I sprinkled you with is magical. You can breathe underwater!"

The turtle turned his head and gave them a

big smile. Jasmine, Summer and Ellie let their breath go and grinned as they found they could breathe easily.

They held on tight as the turtle swam deeper and deeper. Soon they could see a beautiful underwater town on the sandy seabed in front of them. Tiny houses with delicate coral spires and pearly shell roofs peeped out from between the rocks. All around the city was a

beautiful coral reef, and at the top of the reef
rose the turrets of a castle.

"That must be Mermaid Reef," Ellie breathed.

The turtle nodded and came to a smooth stop.

"We'll have to swim the rest of the way,"
Trixi called.

"Thanks for the lift!" Summer said as the girls hopped off the turtle's great green shell.

The turtle waved a fin and turned to swim back up to the surface.

"Wheeee!" Ellie giggled as she bobbed about, floating up a little then flapping her arms to bring herself down again. "This is fun!"

Trixi and the girls swam towards the town happily, chasing one another around the sea plants and rocks. Summer squealed when she noticed a tiny pink seahorse bobbing in the seaweed, its delicate tail curled round a long stem.

"She's so pretty," Summer said, reaching out to stroke the tiny seahorse's head.

"Me?" the little seahorse asked, blushing a deeper shade of pink.

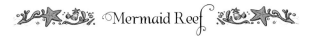

Summer gasped in delight. The seahorse could understand her!

"It's the bubble dust," Trixi explained with a smile. "Its magic allows you to enjoy all underwater life."

"I'm Rosie," said the pink seahorse, her fins rippling in the current.

"Have you noticed anything strange around here, Rosie?" asked Trixi. "We think that one of Queen Malice's thunderbolts might be hidden in Mermaid Reef. We have to get to the city and see if we can spot it."

"I'll show you the quickest way there," the little seahorse said.

The girls followed Rosie through the reef and they soon arrived at a coral gateway that led to the underwater town. As they approached, an enormous octopus climbed over the top of the arch, glaring at them with big, beady eyes.

Ellie jumped in fright, but the octopus just lifted a tentacle and waved them through. Then it clambered back over the gate to sit next to a huge pink pearl that was resting in a giant oyster

shell at the top of the entrance.

"The octopus looks after the wishing pearl," explained Rosie as they swam along. "It's the most precious object in the entire ocean. It can grant any wish you make."

"Meeting a real-life mermaid will be like a wish coming true." Ellie sighed as they swam further into the town, where little shell houses were hidden among the vibrant plants and colourful seaweed. "I thought we'd have seen some by now!"

"Mermaids can make themselves invisible," Trixi told her. "So they may be around, you just might not be able to see them!"

"Does that mean there might be mermaids in our world too? Jasmine asked excitedly.

"Maybe," Trixi replied with a little smile. The girls looked at one another in amazement.

"Most of the merpeople will be in Coral

Castle today," Rosie told them. "It's just up ahead." She nodded at a castle that was rising out of the reef in front of them. It had tall coral towers and was decorated with thousands of shimmery pearls and shells.

"That's where Lady Merlana, the leader of the mermaids, lives," the little seahorse continued. "Every year she holds a singing contest called the Sound of the Sea Competition. All the merpeople will be there."

"Then what are we waiting for?" Jasmine grinned. "Let's go!"

Rosie led them through the castle's huge doors and then down a shell-lined corridor into a massive hall.

The girls gazed in wonder at the sight in front of them. The hall was full of hundreds of mermaids and mermen!

"It's the final round of the competition

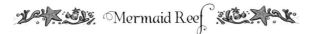

tonight," Rosie explained. "The winner gets to make a wish on the wishing pearl, they can ask for anything they want."

"I wish we could stay and watch the show," Summer sighed. "But we have to find the thunderbolt before it causes any trouble."

"Actually, I think I've found it!" Ellie cried, pointing to a black shard sticking out of the coral by one of the seats. It was the spiky tip of Queen Malice's thunderbolt!

"Oh, no!" exclaimed Jasmine, "Queen Malice must be trying to ruin the competition!"

"I think we had better find Lady Merlana," said Trixi. "She needs to know what's going on."

Rosie led Jasmine, Summer, Ellie and Trixi to the stage. There was a ripple of noise as the merfolk caught sight of the girls' legs!

They swam backstage and stopped outside a door with 'Lady Merlana' written on it in curly writing.

Ellie knocked on the door and it swung open.

Inside was beautiful mermaid with long, flowing blonde hair and a sparkling silver tail. Lady Merlana turned and noticed them floating there. Her bright eyes widened with surprise. "Visitors from the Other Realm !" she gasped. "How wonderful!" Just then she noticed Trixi and Rosie swimming beside the girls and smiled. "Trixi! How lovely to see you again!

Is King Merry with you?"

"I'm afraid not, Lady
Merlana," Trixi
replied. "But I'm
sure he'll arrive
soon." She turned
to the girls. "This is
Summer, Ellie and
Jasmine. They've
been helping to stop
Queen Malice's mean
magic. I'm afraid we think
she's going to try and wreck the Sound of the
Sea Competition."

"We found one of her thunderbolts in the
castle hall," added Ellie.

Lady Merlana looked confused. "Well,
everything is going fine so far. The show is
almost ready to begin."

The girls looked at one another worriedly. Queen Malice's nasty thunderbolts always caused trouble. The horrid queen was sure to be up to something!

"Maybe we should see if the other judges have noticed anything funny," Lady Merlana suggested. "I'll give them a call." She picked up a conch shell from her dressing table and put it up to her ear.

"We use those shells to hear the sea in our world!" exclaimed Ellie as Lady Merlana murmured into the shell.

"They work even better underwater," Trixi said. "You can hear from one shell to another!"

A couple of minutes later two breathtakingly beautiful mermaids and a

handsome merman arrived.

"Girls, this is Cordelia, Meredith and Zale," Lady Merlana said as she pointed to the merfolk.

"Nice to meet you," Summer said with a smile.

The girls all felt a bit awkward in front of such glamorous merfolk, especially when they were still in their school uniforms, but the merpeople seemed delighted to meet them.

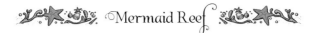

"I've always wanted to see a real-life human!" exclaimed Meredith.

"Wonderful to meet you," beamed Zale.

Cordelia and Meredith swam forward to hug Summer and Jasmine, and Zale floated over to shake Ellie's hand.

Cordelia was very excited, and kept comparing her tail to Summer's legs, looking at her feet and tickling her toes.

Summer giggled and shyly reached out to touch the mermaid's lilac tail. It was covered with tiny scales, just like a fish!

Suddenly, there was a loud clap of thunder, and all the mermaids disappeared in a cloud of bubbles!

"What happened?" gasped Lady Merlana.

"I'll try to magic the judges

back," Trixi said. She tapped her ring, but nothing happened. She shook her head sadly. "If my magic won't work, this definitely has something to do with the queen's thunderbolt."

"The competition is due to start any minute!" Lady Merlana cried, flicking her tail anxiously. "What am I going to do without my judges?"

Just then the girls saw a blue and white polka-dotted submarine moving backwards over the sand, outside the castle. Through the porthole

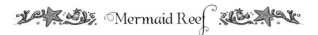

they could see a small, round man sitting inside. He was peering through the boat's periscope with a confused look on his face.

"It's King Merry!" Summer cried.

Trixi tapped her ring and in a flash the submarine came to a halt and the king swam out, his half-moon spectacles perched wonkily on his nose. His crown was balanced on top of a large round diver's helmet that looked a like an upside-down goldfish bowl!

Trixi helped him take his helmet off, then burst a purple bubble over him so that he could breathe under the water.

King Merry gave a huge sneeze that blew his glasses off his nose and onto the sand.

Lady Merlana scooped them

up and gave them back to him. "Welcome, Your Majesty," she said. "We're glad you've come to see the show."

"I'm looking forward to it," he replied cheerily. "Hello, girls," the king said, smiling at Ellie, Summer and Jasmine. "Have you come to watch the show, too?"

"They've come to find another one of Queen Malice's thunderbolts," said Trixi. "And there might not be a show unless we find the judges! The thunderbolt has made them disappear."

"Oh, dear!" King Merry sighed, looking very worried.

"At Unicorn Valley and Cloud Island, things went back to normal once we'd broken Queen Malice's spell," Summer pointed out. "So if we make sure her nasty magic doesn't wreck the competition, then the judges should reappear."

"You're right," agreed Ellie.

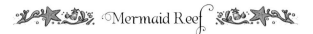

Trixi nodded. "That makes sense. Queen Malice just wants to keep them out of the way so the competition will be ruined."

"But it will be ruined if the judges aren't here," replied Lady Merlana sadly.

"Couldn't someone else judge the acts?" asked Ellie.

"I know," suggested Trixi. "You girls can help! Jasmine is great at singing and dancing and Ellie makes fantastic clothes, so she can judge the costumes. And Summer is brilliant with words, so she can judge the songwriting."

The girls all stared at her with their mouths wide open.

"Us?" Summer squeaked.

"Why not?" asked Trixi. "You'd be perfect!"

King Merry and Rosie nodded their heads in agreement.

"What a splendid idea," Lady Merlana said

approvingly. "Will you help us?"

"Of course!" the girls cried together.

Lady Merlana smiled and led them over to the stage.

"I'm not sure about this," Summer whispered to Ellie. "The merpeople are expecting to see three glamorous judges. What are they going to think of us in our school uniforms?"

"I can fix that," Trixi said. She tapped her ring and instantly their school uniforms were transformed into beautiful outfits. Summer had a long yellow dress, Jasmine wore a sparkly pink top with black leggings and Ellie had a shimmery emerald-green dress with purple swirls on it.

"There you go!" Trixi said, looking very pleased with herself.

"You all look beautiful," Rosie told them shyly.

Jasmine, Ellie and Summer were delighted. Now they couldn't wait for the show to start! They trod water backstage while Trixi, Rosie and King Merry floated over to find their seats amongst the merpeople in the audience.

Finally, the shell curtains opened and Lady Merlana swam onto the stage. "Mermaids and mermen," she announced. "We have some very special guests to judge the Sound of the Sea Competition this year, all the way from the Other Realm."

The girls grinned with excitement. It was time for the contest to begin!

Summer, Jasmine and Ellie felt very important as the merpeople whispered and stared, some of

them floating up off their seats so they could get a better look at the humans' legs!

The girls smiled and waved as they took their places in front of the stage.

As soon as they sat down, the shell-curtains opened again and Lady Merlana announced the first contestant, a golden-haired mermaid called Nerissa.

Nerissa sang a haunting song about a

lonely sea witch. As she sang,
tears started to roll down
her cheeks, transforming
into beautiful pearls that
floated around her. When
the song ended the pearls
glowed before disappearing
in a flash.

The audience clapped and
cheered, thumping their tails
down on the seabed. Summer,
Jasmine and Ellie jumped up to
give Nerissa a standing ovation.

Next, Lady Merlana announced
Atlanta, a red-haired mermaid with a
shimmering lilac tail and a blue seaweed
top. She was joined by four angelfish with
long tails. They danced around her as she
sang a soft melody.

Next up was a handsome merman called Orcan, with blond hair and a dashing silver tail. He sang a soulful song that made the sea seem calmer. Halfway through the performance, the girls heard the distant sound of whalesong, which got louder and louder! Jasmine turned around and caught her breath – through the window she could see a gigantic blue whale,

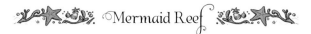

who had joined in with Orcan's song, turning it
into a magical duet!

"That was incredible!" Summer gasped,
clapping in delight as the gentle whale grinned
at her.

The audience was thrilled. Once again they
cheered and thumped their tails down on the
seabed as the merman bowed, then left the stage.

"Brilliant!" declared Jasmine. "How are we
going to choose a winner?"

Finally the last contestant, Nerin, came onto
the stage. She was a tiny mermaid but to
everyone's amazement, her voice was so
powerful that it made the waves lash wildly
above the castle, rocking everyone from side
to side.

Suddenly the sea seemed to go dark. Nerin's
voice trailed off as the water got darker.

"Wh-what's that?" Summer asked, pointing

out of the bubble windows.

A dark shape lurked overhead. As it got closer, the girls saw that it was a large black boat with an anchor shaped like a thunderbolt.

"It's Queen Malice's yacht!" King Merry cried in alarm.

Summer felt a chill run through her as a

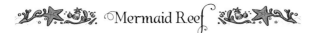

shadowy figure with spiky hair and bat-like
wings dropped out of the yacht and down into
the water. Then another and another.

"Oh, no!" she shouted in horror. "It's the Storm
Sprites!"

The sprites were wearing diving masks and
snorkels. They swam along awkwardly, their
leathery wings struggling through the water, as
they headed towards the entrance to the reef.

"They're after the wishing pearl!" Summer realised with a gasp.

"Don't worry," said Lady Merlana confidently. "My octopus guard will stop them."

Sure enough, as the Storm Sprites approached, the octopus appeared at the top of the gateway and wrapped its tentacles protectively around the oyster shell.

But suddenly a thunderbolt burst out from Queen Malice's yacht like a torpedo. A loud crash echoed through the water and the octopus disappeared in a cloud of bubbles, just like the judges had.

Lady Merlana cried out and started swimming towards the arch. Trixi and the girls set off behind her as King Merry and Rosie watched in horror.

The girls swam as quickly as they could, but their legs couldn't keep up with Merlana's fins.

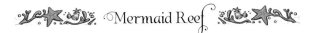

"She's not going to reach the pearl in time!" Jasmine shouted to the others as they swam.

"That pearl is very powerful," Trixi cried. "If Queen Malice gets hold of it, she'll be able to wish for all kinds of horrible things!"

Ellie stopped swimming. "We'll never catch up," she cried. "But we have to do something!"

"How about trapping the sprites?" Jasmine

suggested. "Could you magic up a big bubble?"

"That might work," Trixi said thoughtfully.

"Quick!" shouted Ellie as the lead sprite reached out his spiky fingers for the pearl.

Trixi tapped her ring and suddenly each sprite was surrounded by a sparkling bubble. The silly creatures shouted and banged their flippers against the walls.

"That should stop them long enough for Lady Merlana to get the pearl," Trixi said. "Come on!"

Lady Merlana looked at the sprites inside the bubbles in amazement. Then with a flick of her tail she reached the wishing pearl, which was still lying in the giant oyster shell at the top of the gateway.

"We've got to hurry!" gasped Summer, swimming up behind her. "The sprites won't be trapped for long. We have to hide the pearl!"

"But where can we hide it?" Jasmine asked as she arrived, out of breath.

"You can't," came a voice from above them.

The girls gasped in horror as Queen Malice appeared overhead, riding on top of a gigantic black stingray, and snatched the wishing pearl from its shell.

"Ha!" Queen Malice gave a triumphant laugh. "It's mine and there's nothing you can do!"

As the girls watched in dismay, she held the pearl high above her head and cried, "I wish I was the ruler of the Secret Kingdom, and all my subjects obeyed me!"

Queen Malice laughed wickedly as she put her hands up to her head to touch the pointy crown that now rested there – it was King Merry's one!

The sprites burst their bubbles and paddled over to Queen Malice, cheering.

Queen Malice turned to look at Lady Merlana

and Trixi. "Greet your ruler!" she demanded.

Lady Merlana gave a deep bow, and Trixi flew up to Queen Malice and curtsied to her.

"How can I serve you, Your Majesty?" the little pixie asked in a strange, blank voice.

Summer gasped. "What's happening?" she whispered to Jasmine and Ellie. "Why are Trixi and Lady Merlana doing what she says?"

"It must be the wish," Ellie said. "We seem to be the only ones who aren't affected."

"I think it's because we're not from the Secret Kingdom," Summer said. "So we're not her subjects!"

Queen Malice turned to look at them.

Suddenly Jasmine dropped into a deep curtsy. "Your Royal Highness," she said, turning her head and winking at her friends.

"Everyone follow me back to the yacht," snapped Queen Malice.

"Yes, my queen," Lady Merlana and Trixi chanted, as if they were hypnotised.

"Yes, my queen," the girls copied.

Queen Malice's stingray started swimming up towards the yacht. Ellie, Summer and Jasmine followed along behind Trixi, Lady Merlana and the Storm Sprites.

"Good idea, Jasmine," Ellie whispered. "Now she thinks her wish has affected us, too!"

The girls looked ahead at Queen Malice, who was wishing for more and more things. They watched as she passed a jewelled coronet and a pair of diamond shoes back for the Storm Sprites to carry. Next she passed the pearl to the sprite behind her.

"We've got to get that pearl back!" Summer said determinedly.

"I have an idea," Ellie said. "Follow my lead!"

She, Jasmine and Summer swam quickly to

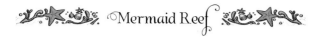

catch up with the lead sprite.

"You're so lucky to be Queen Malice's servant," Ellie said to the sprite enviously.

"Yeah," Jasmine joined in. "I wish we could do something to help her."

The sprite looked pleased. "Oh, we've got loads of jobs that you can do!" he laughed nastily. "You can cook the bats' breakfast and feed the stink toads."

"Hurry up, back there!" Queen Malice snarled.

"I could swim a lot faster without all of this stuff…" the sprite nearest to Summer grumbled as he dragged along a treasure chest that was overflowing with jewels. He glanced at Summer. "I know. You can carry it all!" He dumped the heavy box into Summer's arms gleefully.

The other sprites laughed.

"Good idea!" one chuckled as he passed a huge mirror to Ellie. "You can take this."

"Yeah!" said the lead sprite. "And this too!" He passed Jasmine the wishing pearl.

Jasmine gasped at she looked down at the wishing pearl. The sprite suddenly realised his mistake and reached for it, but it was too late.

"I wish all Queen Malice's wishes were undone and she was far away from here!" Jasmine shouted quickly.

"Noooooooo!" Queen Malice shouted, trying to hold onto King Merry's crown as a vast whirlpool started twirling around her, twisting it away from her grasping fingers. The Storm Sprites were sucked into the whirlpool too!

"You haven't won!" Queen Malice screeched as she spun further into the watery hole. "One day I will rule the kingdom… Just you wait and seeeeeeee!"

All at once the whirlpool disappeared, and the girls were left floating next to Lady Merlana and Trixi, who were shaking their heads as if they were waking up from a bad dream.

Jasmine turned to Lady Merlana and handed her the wishing pearl. "I think this belongs to you," she grinned.

"You've saved us!" cried Lady Merlana, hugging the girls.

As they swam back into Mermaid Reef, King

Merry and Rosie swam over to the girls. Ellie handed the king his crown.

"Thank you very much!" he cried happily, popping it back on his head.

Rosie bobbed up to Summer, who held out her little finger so that the seahorse could curl her tail around it.

"Yes, thank you," Lady Merlana said to the girls as she cradled the precious wishing pearl carefully in her arms. "You've saved the Secret Kingdom once again!"

"We still need to break Queen Malice's thunderbolt to get the judges back," Ellie reminded her.

Lady Merlana put her hands to her mouth in surprise. "I almost forgot!" she gasped. "We have to finish the Sound of the Sea Competition!"

Lady Merlana led everyone back to Coral Castle. The girls huddled together at the table to discuss the acts. They all agreed that Nerissa, the mermaid whose tears turned to pearls, and Orcan, the merman who sang with the whale, were the best acts. But they just couldn't decide who was better.

"I know!" said Ellie, thinking hard.

She told her idea to Summer and Jasmine, who both nodded happily. Then she floated over to Lady Merlana and whispered in her ear.

Lady Merlana floated to the centre of the stage. A hush fell over the audience.

"Mermaids and mermen," she started. "All our contestants deserve a big round of applause!"

The hall filled with claps and cheers.

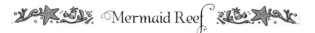

Lady Merlana put her hands to her mouth in surprise. "I almost forgot!" she gasped. "We have to finish the Sound of the Sea Competition!"

Lady Merlana led everyone back to Coral Castle. The girls huddled together at the table to discuss the acts. They all agreed that Nerissa, the mermaid whose tears turned to pearls, and Orcan, the merman who sang with the whale, were the best acts. But they just couldn't decide who was better.

"I know!" said Ellie, thinking hard.

She told her idea to Summer and Jasmine, who both nodded happily. Then she floated over to Lady Merlana and whispered in her ear.

Lady Merlana floated to the centre of the stage. A hush fell over the audience.

"Mermaids and mermen," she started. "All our contestants deserve a big round of applause!"

The hall filled with claps and cheers.

"Ellie, Summer and Jasmine have made a decision," Lady Merlana continued, "…and… we have a draw!" she declared. "The winners are Nerissa and Orcan."

The audience cheered wildly as Lady Merlana put garlands of colourful sea anemones around the winners' necks, then presented each of them with a starfish medal.

Suddenly there was a loud cracking sound.

"It sounds like the
thunderbolt has
broken!" gasped Ellie.

There was a burst
of bubbles and the
judges appeared in
front of them, looking
a little dazed.

"Have we missed the
competition?" Cordelia
asked worriedly.

Lady Merlana explained how the girls had
taken their places and stopped Queen Malice
from stealing the wishing pearl.

"Oh, thank you!" Cordelia cried. "You saved
the day!"

"There's one more thing you simply have
to see," said Lady Merlana as she beckoned
the winning acts over. She turned to the singers

and smiled. "It's time for you to make a wish on the pearl," she told them.

Everyone gathered around as Nerissa and Orcan floated in front of the magic pearl. They both looked thoughtful for a moment, and then Nerissa leaned over and whispered something in Orcan's ear.

Orcan smiled and nodded.

"We'd like to give our wish to Jasmine, Ellie and Summer," Nerissa said with a smile. "If it

weren't for them, the wishing pearl would still be in Queen Malice's hands!"

Jasmine, Ellie and Summer gasped in surprise.

"Whatever are we going to wish for?" Ellie asked.

"I know what I'd like," Summer said shyly. "I'd love to see how it feels to be a mermaid!"

Jasmine and Ellie grinned. What a brilliant idea!

"We wish that we could be mermaids – just for a little while," Jasmine said.

The wishing pearl glowed brightly.

Ellie shut her eyes, and when she opened them she saw that she had a gorgeous orangey-red tail that matched her hair! She looked over and saw that Summer now had a pretty seaweed green tail, and Jasmine had a shimmering silver one.

"We're mermaids!" Ellie cried, flicking her tail and somersaulting in excitement.

The girls spent the rest of the day swimming about, chasing the other mermaids around and playing hide and seek – it was such fun!

But all too soon the wish wore off. "We should probably go now," Jasmine said reluctantly.

Lady Merlana hugged them all. "I've got a gift for you," she said, holding out a beautiful silver pearl. It looked like a small version of the wishing pearl.

"You can use it to turn invisible, just like

merpeople do." She handed it to Jasmine – who
promptly disappeared. "This is brilliant," Jasmine
giggled as she invisibly tickled Summer and Ellie.

"The magic doesn't last for long," Lady
Merlana warned them. "But hopefully it will
help you fight Queen Malice's horrible magic."

Trixi, Rosie and King Merry rushed over

to say goodbye too.

"You will come back soon, won't you?" King Merry asked worriedly. "There are still two more thunderbolts hidden in the kingdom."

"Of course we will," Jasmine told him. "We'll come whenever you need us."

The girls waved goodbye to their new friends

as Trixi tapped her ring and transported them back to the human world.

A few seconds later they found themselves back in the girls' toilet at school, as if they'd never left.

"I'm glad time has stood still," Jasmine said, "because I'm really hungry!"

The lid on the Magic Box sprang open, and Jasmine carefully put the special pearl in one of the empty compartments.

"I wonder where we'll go for our next adventure," said Summer.

"I don't mind where it is." Ellie smiled. "But I do hope it's soon!"

Magic Mountain

Magic Mountain

"I'm Queen Malice!" cried the girl in black.
"Get them, Storm Sprites!"

Two small creatures ran into the room.

Summer Hammond and Ellie Macdonald ran away, giggling. The girl in black was only their friend Jasmine and the little Storm Sprites were Summer's brothers!

Soon it was time for Summer's step-dad to give the boys a bath.

"But I want to be a Storm Sprite," whined three-year-old Finn.

"Storm Sprites aren't real, silly," five-year-old Connor told him scornfully as they headed into the bathroom.

Summer grinned at Jasmine and Ellie. Little did the boys know that Storm Sprites were real, and that they lived in a magical land called the Secret Kingdom!

The kingdom was a wonderful place but it was in trouble – and only Ellie, Summer and Jasmine could help.

One day, the girls had found a box at a school jumble sale. The magical box was created by King Merry, the ruler of the Secret Kingdom. King Merry and his royal pixie, Trixi, had asked the girls for their help in stopping Queen Malice, the king's mean sister, from causing trouble in the kingdom.

Queen Malice had been so angry when King Merry had been chosen to rule the Secret Kingdom instead of her that she had hidden six horrible thunderbolts around the land. The thunderbolts would cause chaos and ruin all the fun in the kingdom.

Jasmine, Ellie and Summer had already found

four of the thunderbolts and broken their nasty spells. But there were still two more to find!

The girls headed up to Summer's room to watch a DVD. Her room was painted a soft yellow and had lots of animal posters all over the walls. Summer put on her comfy old yellow flowered pyjamas, Ellie got into her green-and-purple pair and then they both admired Jasmine's shorts and vest set, which were brand new and covered with big pink polka dots.

Jasmine and Ellie took the Magic Box down from Summer's tall bookcase and put it on top of Ellie's sleeping bag. The box had wooden sides carved with pictures of magical creatures. A mirror was set into its curved lid, which was surrounded by six beautiful green gemstones.

The girls stared at the box, willing a message to appear, but nothing happened. "It's no good!" Jasmine laughed, "let's put a film on."

Summer put a DVD in, and the girls ended up laughing so much that Mrs Hammond had to come in and tell them it was bedtime. After that they talked in whispers for a while, then one by one they drifted off to sleep.

In the middle of the night, Summer suddenly woke up. Her room was lit up by a dim glow.

But it can't be morning already, she thought. She glanced up at her shelves and her heart jumped with excitement – the light was coming

from the Magic Box! She slipped out of bed and nudged Ellie and Jasmine.

"The Magic Box," she whispered. "It's glowing!"

Ellie and Jasmine woke up and quickly scrambled out of their sleeping bags.

As the girls gathered around the box, words began to form in the mirror on its lid:

"Where the brownies slide, not run,
Where they ride on boards for fun,
Where cheeks are red and breath is white,
That's where you must go tonight!"

"Surfing brownies?" whispered Summer uncertainly.

"Surfing isn't the only sport that uses a board," said Ellie thoughtfully. "My uncle went snowboarding last month."

"And when it's cold and snowy, you can see your breath and your cheeks go red!" Jasmine cried loudly.

"Shhh!" Summer told her, giggling. "You'll wake up my mum!"

"Sorry," Jasmine whispered as quietly as she could. "We must be going where there are snowboarding brownies!"

"Look, the Magic Box is opening," said Ellie.

The girls watched as the lid of the box opened. Ellie reached carefully inside, took out the magical map of the kingdom that King Merry had given them on their first visit. She spread it out on her sleeping bag.

"What about here?" Ellie pointed. At the very bottom of the Secret Kingdom was a huge mountain, capped with sparkly pink snow!

"It's called Magic Mountain," said Summer, reading the label underneath the moving image.

The girls put their palms on the beautiful green stones. Jasmine leaned down to whisper the answer to the riddle.

"Magic Mountain."

Everything was silent for a moment, but then Summer's curtains twitched and a tiny pixie flew into Summer's bedroom, riding on a leaf! Her dress was made out of little green leaves, neatly stitched together. She wore a cape, and a ring twinkled on her finger like a star in the night.

"It's Trixibelle!" Summer whispered delightedly.

Trixi tapped her ring and the string of lights hanging at the top of Summer's curtains lit up the room with a pretty pink glow.

"We've worked out where the next thunderbolt is, Trixi," Summer told their tiny pixie friend excitedly. "It's at Magic Mountain!"

"We must go at once," said the little pixie. She looked at the girls. "Oh, but you can't go dressed like that! Stand still for a moment."

There was a brief flash and a tinkling sound. The girls looked down to find themselves wearing coats,

boots, scarves, gloves and earmuffs, all the same colours as their pyjamas! On their heads were the sparkly tiaras that magically appeared every time they visited the Secret Kingdom. These showed that the girls were Very Important Friends of King Merry's.

"Perfect," Trixi said approvingly. "Now we're ready for snow!"

Trixi tapped her ring to summon the magical whirlwind that would transport them all to the Secret Kingdom, and chanted:

"The evil queen has trouble planned.
Brave helpers fly to save our land!"

Ellie closed her eyes as the three friends were whisked through the air. As the wind died down, she opened them and saw that they were right at the top of the snow-covered mountain they'd seen on the map. She could see a town far off in the distance at the base of the mountain, but it looked tiny from so high up.

It was already dawn in the Secret Kingdom, and the sun was starting to rise gently above the mountaintops, making the pink snowflakes twinkle in the air.

"It's so beautiful!" Jasmine gasped.

"Are we going all the way down there?" Summer asked, pointing towards the town.

"Yes," said Trixi with a smile. "But don't worry – it won't take long at all!" She tapped her ring and suddenly each girl had a pair of skis strapped to her feet. Summer's were yellow, Jasmine's were pink and Ellie's purple.

"Wheeee!" cried Jasmine, pushing off with her ski poles and sliding down the hill.

"Jasmine, come back!" shouted Ellie in alarm. "I can't ski!"

"Don't worry," said Trixi. "I'll put a spell on your skis so that they carry you safely down the slope." She pointed her ring towards the girls' feet and a burst of glitter settled over their skis.

Summer gave Ellie a gentle push and then set off down the hill behind her. It was a bit scary, but the magic skis worked wonderfully! Soon Ellie and Summer drew level with Jasmine.

As the girls skied along next to one another, they looked around in wonder. Summer saw a herd of reindeer galloping through the sky towards a distant wood. Their hooves gave off

sparks of magic as they flew through the air.

"I never thought I'd actually get to see flying reindeer!" Ellie grinned.

The girls skied all the way down the

mountain into the town below. It was a perfect
winter scene, with beautiful snow-covered houses
and cafés laid out around a square. There were
even pretty little igloos, glittering pink, just like
the snow they were made from.

"The cafés look like snowballs!" Ellie giggled.

But as Summer looked around the pretty town, she got a funny feeling. "Where is everyone?" she asked warily.

The snowball cafés were shut and several snowboards, sleds and skis had been left lying outside as if they'd been abandoned in a hurry. Wind whistled eerily all around the mountainside. "It's usually a lot busier than this," said Trixi, who was flying along beside the girls.

"It must have something to do with Queen Malice's thunderbolt," Jasmine said. "We'd better see if we can find it."

They carried on, skiing down a slope that was lined with realistic-looking ice sculptures. There were reindeer, penguins, seals and even a big polar bear.

"Hey!" said Jasmine. She pointed at one of the ice statues and frowned. "I'm sure that penguin just waved its wing at me!"

"I expect it did," Trixi smiled. "Those statues are magical. The snow brownies make them. It's because of the brownies that Magic Mountain is such a fun place to visit."

The girls hurried over to take a closer look.

"Hello!" said Ellie, shaking the polar bear's frozen paw.

The bear moved his head from side to side. He seemed to be looking for something.

"Are you wondering where all the brownies have gone?" asked Jasmine.

The statue nodded slowly in reply.

"Don't worry," Summer told him. "We'll find out what's going on."

As the girls skied onwards, Summer teeth began to chatter. Even with her cosy clothes on, she was still very cold. "Maybe the snow brownies are off somewhere keeping warm."

"But shouldn't snow brownies like the cold?" Jasmine asked.

"They do," Trixi agreed. "But when it gets too cold the snow turns to ice, and so do the snow brownies. They wear ember necklaces to keep them warm. They even use everwarm ember coals to heat the igloos and cafes. The embers are magical – they keep everyone warm but don't make the snow melt."

Jasmine shivered. "I think we need to find some everwarm ember necklaces to warm ourselves up!"

"I know!" Trixi said with a smile. "Let's go

and see King Merry at his winter palace. He might know where everyone is. Every winter he comes skiing at Magic Mountain, even though he's not very good at it." She winked at the girls.

"Last year he fell over so much he caused an avalanche!" she added with a giggle.

Ellie, Summer and Jasmine smiled. They were always glad to see the friendly king – and they would be very pleased indeed to get out of the freezing cold!

On their way to the palace, they skied past a big lake full of very clear ice.

"That's Ice-Skate Lake," said Trixi. " There are always brownies playing on it. I've never seen it empty before."

"I think I know the reason why," Ellie said
grimly. "Look!" She pointed at a snowdrift
beside the lake. There, sticking out of it, was
Queen Malice's horrible black thunderbolt!

"Come on," said Jasmine as they looked at
the jagged black shape. "Let's find King Merry
and figure out a way to break this nasty
thunderbolt."

It wasn't long before the girls saw the beautiful
royal building ahead. The palace had one big
central tower surrounded by six smaller ones
that were connected to
it by delicate
walkways of
sparkling
frost. Dozens
of windows
shaped like

snowflakes dotted the walls, each with a dusting
of snow on the windowsill.

Trixi knocked on the front door, which was
shaped like a giant snowflake.

"Where is everyone?" fretted Trixi after a
moment or two. She pointed her ring at the
door, chanting:

"These girls are here to save the day,

So don't you try to block their way!"

With a creak the door swung open.

The girls took off their skis and nervously
followed Trixi into the hall. Everything was dark.
Worse still, it was almost as cold in here as it
had been outside!

"King Merry?" Jasmine shouted. Her voice
echoed spookily around the icy walls.

The girls walked along the corridors until
they came to a huge
room full of brownies,
all huddling together
for warmth. In the
middle of them all
was poor King Merry,
shivering hard.

The little king looked
even rounder than usual.

As the girls got closer, they could see why he seemed so tubby – it looked like he was wearing all of his clothes at the same time!

"T-t-trixi! G-girls! I am so h-happy to s-s-see you," the king stuttered, hugging himself and jiggling on the spot.

"You look freezing!" Summer said sympathetically, rubbing King Merry's arm.

"Let me help," Trixi said, flying high over the

shivering brownies. She started casting spells as quickly as she could. Every time she tapped her ring, a hat or a rolled-up blanket or a pair of cosy woollen socks appeared.

The brownies raised their eyes and watched as colourful woolly hats began drifting down from above. There was one for each of them, printed with the brownie's name and a different snowflake pattern.

As they put the warm hats on and snuggled up in the blankets, the brownies started to look

happier and their ears turned bright pink.

"Thank you!" said one brownie. Like his friends, he was about half the girls' height and had pointy ears. His hat had Blizzard written on it. "Have you come to help us? We've been huddling here all night to keep warm. I was afraid we'd turn into ice!"

"We're here to help," said Jasmine, leaning down to talk to him. "Do you know what's happened?"

"It's the everwarm embers," he said, looking up at her worriedly. "They've all gone out!"

He pointed towards a big fireplace on the other side of the room. It was heaped high with dusty-looking grey lumps.

"Even the embers in our necklaces are cold," the brownie said, holding up a long string that was tied around his neck. At the end of it was a dim grey stone.

"And if we get too cold, we'll turn to ice!"
another brownie said.

"Maybe you could make a fire to heat the
embers up?" Ellie suggested to Trixi.

"I'll try," said the little pixie, aiming her ring
at the fireplace. A stream of crackling red sparks
flew out of it and hit the pile of embers, but they
stayed grey and dark.

"That settles it," said Trixi, folding her arms

and looking cross. "If my magic can't fix it, then it must be the work of that nasty thunderbolt."

"The other thunderbolts have always shattered when we've stopped Queen Malice from ruining things," Summer said thoughtfully. "Maybe if we can find a way to relight the everwarm embers, that will break Queen Malice's spell!"

"It's daytime now and it's getting warmer," said Ellie. "Couldn't we just pile the embers up in the sunshine?"

"I'm afraid it wouldn't get hot enough to light them, even when it's sunny," said another brownie, whose hat had Flurry sewn on it.

All of a sudden there was a horrible, cackling laugh outside. The girls peered out through one of the windows. They saw a sleigh, pulled by two wolves with shining red eyes and very big teeth. A tall, shadowy figure was standing in the sleigh, staring at the palace. She had a pointy crown on her head, which was perched on top of a mess of frizzy hair. Her black dress billowed around her in the cold wind as she raised her spiky staff to urge the wolves on.

"It's Queen Malice!" whispered Ellie. "And she's heading this way!" She felt Blizzard's hand creep into hers, and she held it tight.

Queen Malice peered in through the snowflake-shaped windows as the sleigh slid by.

There was a screech of laughter from outside. "It's no use trying to hide, dear brother," Queen Malice called. "I know you're in there! There's nothing you or those annoying girls can do. Soon your precious snow brownies will turn into ice lollies. Then there will be no one to look after Magic Mountain, and no one will be able to have any fun in the snow!"

With a cackle, Queen Malice turned and

pointed her spiky staff at the peak of the
mountain, and shot a bolt of lightning into
the sky. The lightning struck a big grey cloud,
pushing it in front of the sun. The sky turned
dim and grey.

The sled leapt forward and Queen Malice was
carried away.

"If we don't find a way to relight the
everwarm embers soon," Jasmine said with a

shiver, "Magic Mountain will be ruined forever!"

"We have to save the brownies!" Trixi said, shivering so hard her leaf shook.

"If only we had the crystal that the weather imps gave us," said Ellie thoughtfully. "Then we could control the weather and get rid of that snow cloud." She took a step forward – and tripped over something.

"Oops, clumsy clogs!" laughed Jasmine, catching her friend.

"It's the Magic Box," Ellie said, looking at the floor. "I'm sure this wasn't here a moment ago."

"It must have known we needed the crystal!" exclaimed Summer.

The box slowly opened. Ellie lifted out the weather crystal. The magical jewel glowed as Ellie held it tightly and thought about rays of warm sunshine.

Suddenly the throne room grew lighter and warmer as a hole formed in the storm cloud, letting the sun shine through!

"That's better!" Jasmine said as Ellie gently placed the weather crystal back into its space in the Magic Box. With a flash of light and a twinkle the box disappeared.

"Remember, the weather imps told us the crystal's magic won't last for long," Trixi reminded the girls. "We still need to find a way to relight the embers for good!"

"There was something my step-dad taught me when we went camping last year," Summer said thoughtfully. "He showed us a special way to light a fire. It was something to do with sunshine – I wish I could remember what!"

Blizzard and Flurry's faces lit up.

"We can help with that," grinned Blizzard.

The two little brownies stood on either side of Summer. They linked their hands over her head and chanted:

"Brainstorm spell, brainstorm spell,
Summer's thinking very well!"

As they spoke, pink snowflakes appeared and danced around Summer's head.

Summer's eyes lit up, and she jumped to her

feet. "I remember now!" she said. "You can start
a campfire with a magnifying glass. You hold it
in the sunshine and it focuses the sun's power on
one spot so that it gets really hot – hot enough
to start a fire…or relight embers!"

Jasmine frowned. "But wouldn't we need an
incredibly huge magnifying glass?" she asked.

"You can use anything that's really clear,"
Summer replied, "like a lens from someone's
glasses—"

"Or some ice!" Ellie chimed in,
catching on to Summer's idea.
"We could use the ice
from Ice-Skate Lake!"
cried Jasmine.

"Yes, that's perfect!"
said Summer.

The brownies cheered.
"Let's get moving," said

Jasmine. "We have lots to do before the sun disappears behind that nasty storm cloud again!"

By the time the girls and the brownies got to the town square, they had a plan in place.

First, Summer stood in front of everyone and explained her idea to make a giant lens out of ice. Then Jasmine sent teams of brownies off to gather up all the everwarm embers and bring them back to the town square. Finally, Trixi and Ellie led another group of brownies to Ice-Skate Lake to work on making the ice lens.

"How are we going to cut such a big chunk out of the ice?" Ellie asked Trixi.

"That's a job for the brownies!" she replied. "They can sculpt and shape ice, remember?"

When the group reached Ice-Skate Lake, all the brownies except for Blizzard arranged themselves in a circle around the frozen bank.

Blizzard strapped on a pair of skates and skimmed out across the ice, looking very serious. He skated around in a circle, leaving a deep cut in the surface.

The brownies at the edge of the lake began a quiet chant that sounded like gently falling snow. Then there was a loud crack, and the disc of ice broke away from the lake and rose up into the

air. It spun around, slowly changing shape until
it was curved on both sides like the lens of a
magnifying glass.

Trixi pointed her ring at the ice lens, and it
began to float slowly in the direction of the
town square.

When it reached
the town square,
the girls helped
the rest of the
brownies pile the
final embers onto a
heap in the middle
of a big patch of

sunlight streaming through the hole in the cloud.

Trixi pointed her ring at the floating ice lens
and moved it through the air until it hovered
between the sun and the pile of embers. They
had to get the lens in exactly the right position,

or the plan wouldn't work. They turned it left and right and tilted it backwards and forwards.

All the brownies huddled together anxiously as they looked up at the hole in the snow cloud, which was getting smaller every minute. Any moment now, the weather crystal's magic would wear off and the snow cloud would cover the sun again!

Then, as Trixi tilted the slab of ice to the left, the sunlight finally beamed through its centre. Sunshine streamed onto the embers, bathing them in heat.

"It's working!" Jasmine gasped.

Just as she finished speaking, there was a soft pop. A bright red glow appeared at the very top of the big pile. The first ember was alight!

Another followed, then another and another.

Trixi flew around the edge of the pile a few times, holding her hands out in the warm air.

Once she had warmed up, she tapped her
ring and conjured up an enormous mug full of
steaming hot chocolate for everyone! Each mug
had a sparkly magic marshmallow the size of a
fairy cake in it!

By now the entire pile of embers was shining
red and yellow with heat.

"Look!" said Summer, pointing up at the
afternoon sky. "The reindeer are coming back!"

The magnificent herd flew in low over the pile of embers, warming their bellies.

"Watch out!" one called as he swooped by.

"What do you mean?" called Jasmine, but the reindeer had already flown away.

Then the girls heard an enormous crack! that

echoed around the valley.

"What was that?" Ellie asked her friends.

"I think it was Queen Malice's thunderbolt breaking!" said Jasmine, racing towards the lake to look.

Ellie, Summer, Trixi and the brownies followed behind. When they got to the spot where the thunderbolt had been, all they could see were little black shards scattered on the pink snow.

"We've broken the spell!" Jasmine cried.

A huge shout rose from the crowd of brownies. They all hugged one another, then came forward to take their necklaces from the pile.

Blizzard gave

necklaces to Jasmine, Summer and Ellie, and the girls put them on, smiling as they felt the heat of the ember warming them.

Suddenly there was a cackle of laughter. As everyone looked up, they saw a group of Storm Sprites snowboarding down the mountain towards them, holding buckets full of water.

"We're going to soak those silly everwarm embers and put them out for good!"one sprite called down.

"Oh, no!" Flurry gasped. "If the embers get wet before they're up to full strength, we might never be able to light them again!"

"Don't worry!" Blizzard grinned. "I know how to handle this." He scooped up an armful of snow and a moment later there was a neat pile of snowballs on the ground. Blizzard picked one up and threw it at the nearest sprite, hitting him right on the nose!

"Good idea!" Summer giggled.

Everyone started to pick up snowballs and hurl them at the sprites. Even Trixi joined in, using her pixie magic to send snowballs flying towards the nasty creatures, and knocking three

of them over with one blast from her ring.

Flurry gave a low whistle, and seconds later the flying reindeer landed in the square. He and some other brownies jumped on their backs.

Summer and Jasmine threw one more snowball each and then ran over to the waiting animals. Ellie decided to stay where she was.

"Go ahead and climb up," one of the reindeer told Summer with a smile.

"Thank you!" Summer breathed, gently stroking his velvety nose. She quickly clambered up onto his strong back and wrapped her arms around his neck.

"This is going to be great!" Jasmine said as she climbed up on another reindeer. The animals cantered up into the air.

"Take that!" Jasmine shouted gleefully as she pelted a Storm Sprite from above.

"And that!" Summer joined in, flying nearby.

The sprite squealed as the snowballs rained down from above.

Ellie saw her chance, throwing a snowball that hit him right in his middle. "And THAT!" she yelled triumphantly.

The sprite fell over and dropped his bucket, splashing water everywhere.

"Get out of my way, Big-Ears!" shouted another sprite snowboarding behind him.

As the girls watched, the two sprites started rolling down the hill in a tangle of skinny arms and legs, collecting more and more snow.

The snowball continued to tumble down the mountain, rolling over sprites as it went. It gradually began to slow down as it crossed the town square, and then it landed in a big heap a few metres from the pile of everwarm embers.

Ellie, Trixi, King Merry and the brownies cheered. Summer and Jasmine's reindeer flew in circles to celebrate, then landed gently.

Summer, Jasmine and Blizzard ran over to the others.

"That was amazing!" Summer grinned.

The girls all looked at the sprites. They were still lying in a pile of snow, looking very dizzy. "We'll make sure they can't bother us any more," Blizzard said with a grin.

He and the other snow brownies formed a circle around the sprites, then started their low chanting again. Suddenly pink icicles formed on the sprites' noses and their bony fingers!

"We're turning them into ice statues for a little while," Blizzard told the girls. "It won't hurt them, but it should keep them out of mischief!"

Just then they heard a shriek from high up on the mountain slope. The girls looked up and could just make out a dark shape at the mountain's peak. It was Queen Malice's wolf-sled.

"You haven't seen the last of me!" the queen screeched. "I'll ruin all the fun in the Secret Kingdom – just you wait and see!"

And with that, the wolf-sled sped away.

At that moment it suddenly got dark, and fat

pink snowflakes started falling from the sky.

Summer, Ellie and Jasmine rushed around the town, helping the brownies put an everwarm ember in every home, and in all the lanterns around Ice-Skate Lake.

"It doesn't matter how cold it gets now!" Summer said cheerfully. "The everwarm embers will keep everyone nice and cosy!"

Flurry rushed over, beaming happily. "All the embers are in place," he declared. "Would you like to come to a snowball café and have something to eat?" he asked.

Ellie, Summer and Jasmine looked at one another and grinned. "Yes, please!" they all said at the same time.

Soon the girls were snuggled cosily in a café, eating special, warm ice cream puddings that had been magically baked on the embers.

"Look!" Ellie said, pointing outside.

The Storm Sprites had thawed out. As the girls watched, one of them blew a raspberry at them and then they flapped away.

"It's stopped snowing!" Blizzard realised, pointing outside. "Let's go and have some fun!"

All the brownies leapt up and ran outside.

"Come on, girls!" Flurry called as he headed out the door. "Now we can show you just how magical Magic Mountain really is!"

Summer stared around in amazement.

Suddenly there were brownies sledding, skiing and snowboarding everywhere she looked!

"Would you like to try the ice slides?" Trixi asked Jasmine.

"Oh, yes please!" Jasmine cried.

"Follow us," called Blizzard. He led the girls to a wire with lots of funny benches dangling from it. "These will take us up to the ice slides!" he said. He and Jasmine jumped onto the first chair and were whizzed away up the mountain.

Flurry and Ellie sat on the next chair and Summer followed with King Merry. Soon they were all being carried up the mountain towards the ice slides, which twisted down the slopes like giant helter-skelters.

"Woohoo!" Jasmine laughed, jumping straight onto the slide and pushing off. "Here goes!"

Next Blizzard zoomed down, followed by Ellie, who was holding tightly on to Flurry.

King Merry slipped as he
sat down and ended up
going down the slide
bottom-first! Summer
came close behind,
giggling all the way.
After the slide,
Jasmine lay down in
the pink snow and

made an angel shape with her arms and legs. "I'd like to play in the snow every day!" she said happily.

"I don't think I would," said Ellie. "It's been lovely to visit Magic Mountain, but I like being warm!"

"I like everywhere in the Secret Kingdom," said Summer. She yawned. "But right now I'm looking forward to snuggling up in bed."

Trixi looked at the sun, which was getting lower in the sky.

"Yes, I think it's time for you to go home," she agreed.

"Can we come back soon?" said Jasmine hopefully.

"Ooh yes," King Merry replied, nodding so hard his crown slipped down over one eye. "I don't know how I'd handle my frightful sister without you!"

"Ahem!" coughed Blizzard loudly. The little brownie had an icy pink hourglass in his little hand. "King Merry agreed we should give this to you as a thank-you present. It's an icy hourglass. It freezes time for a little while."

"Thank you," said Jasmine, taking the

hourglass. "I'm sure this will be useful during our adventures!"

Ellie, Summer and Jasmine said goodbye to everyone, and then Trixi tapped her ring. A magic whirlwind began to form around them.

When they opened their eyes again, everything was dark and warm. They were wearing their cosy pajamas.

Summer lifted the Magic Box down from her shelf and put it on her bed. It opened and Jasmine carefully slipped the hourglass in next to the weather crystal.

"What a lovely adventure we had," Summer sighed, crawling under her duvet. "And now there's only one thunderbolt left to find. Where do you think we'll go next?"

But there was no reply from her two friends – they were already fast asleep!

Glitter Beach

Glitter Beach

"Hi, Mum! I'm home!"

Ellie Macdonald ran into the kitchen through the back door. She put her bag down on a chair and then opened it carefully. Inside was a magical box!

Ellie and her best friends Summer and Jasmine were the only ones who knew that the box had been made by King Merry, the ruler of a land called the Secret Kingdom, where lots of magical creatures lived. It was a wonderful place, but it was in terrible trouble.

When everyone in the land had decided they wanted kind King Merry to rule the kingdom, his horrid sister Queen Malice had sent six thunderbolts into different parts of the land. Each thunderbolt had the power to cause trouble. Ellie and her friends had promised to help stop the nasty queen. Whenever one of her thunderbolts appeared, they would see a riddle in the lid of the Magic Box. When they had solved it, Ellie, Summer and Jasmine would be whisked away to the kingdom to try to help. They had already had five wonderful adventures!

If only the lid would start glowing, that would mean that it was time for Ellie and her friends to return to the Secret Kingdom. But all she could see was her own reflection, her red curls falling messily around her face.

Ellie carried the box to the hall carefully, heading for the stairs. She caught sight of her mum through the window, tidying up the hanging baskets in the front garden.

"RARRRRR!" With a loud yell, Molly, Ellie's

little sister, jumped out from where she had been hiding beside the hall table.

Ellie almost dropped the box in shock.

Molly whooped. "I made you jump, Ellie!" She was four and looked just like Ellie had when she was little, with red curls and mischievous green eyes. "What's that?" she said curiously, spotting the box in Ellie's arms.

"It's just an old box," Ellie told her hastily. The last thing she wanted was Molly looking in the Magic Box! Inside it were six wooden compartments, and five of them were filled with the special objects Ellie and the others had collected on their adventures. There was a magic moving map of the Secret Kingdom, a tiny silver unicorn horn that let the person holding it talk to animals, a cloud crystal that could control the weather, a pearl that could turn you invisible and an icy hourglass that could freeze

time. If Molly found those things she'd want to know where they had come from and the girls couldn't tell anyone about the Secret Kingdom!

Ellie swooped the box over her sister's head and put it on the table. Then, she started to tickle Molly to distract her.

Just then the front door opened and Mrs Macdonald came in. "Hello, girls. Did you have a good day at school, Ellie?"

"Yes, fine, thanks, Mum. I'm just going up to

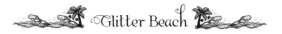

my room for a while."

Grabbing the Magic Box, Ellie quickly ran up the stairs. She changed out of her school clothes and then got out her sketchbook and began to draw a picture of Trixi, the little royal pixie who looked after King Merry.

After a minute she glanced up and almost fell off her chair in surprise.

The box was glowing!

Ellie gasped and jumped to her feet. "Oh wow! It's time for another adventure!"

She threw her school jumper over the box to hide it, and ran downstairs to use

the phone. She had to tell Jasmine and Summer straight away!

"Promise you won't look at the riddle on the box until we get there!" begged Jasmine when Ellie called her.

"I won't!" Ellie promised.

Ellie waited impatiently by the front door. At last she saw Summer running along the street, her blonde pigtails flying out behind her. At the same time Jasmine came racing around the corner on her bike.

The girls all hurried inside. "Hi, girls," Mrs Macdonald called from the kitchen. "Are you staying for tea?"

"Yes, please," Summer and Jasmine both chorused.

"Though hopefully we'll have had an amazing adventure before then!" Jasmine whispered. The girls knew that time in the real

world stayed still when they were in the Secret
Kingdom, so Ellie's mum would never even
notice that they'd been gone. The three friends
shared a smile and raced upstairs.

"Let's see what the riddle says!" Ellie carefully
read out the words that had formed in the
mirror of the box:

"Danger from a royal hand,
A thunderbolt in sparkling sand,

A wicked deed must be put right,
Before the next midsummer night."

Suddenly the box opened and the magic map floated out!

Ellie carefully unfolded it, with Summer and Jasmine peering over her shoulders. Magical pictures on it showed what was happening

on the crescent-shaped island of the Secret
Kingdom, with its emerald green hills and
meadows, aquamarine waters and sandy coves.

"It says 'a thunderbolt in sparkling sand'," said
Summer. "Well, you get sand at the seaside – so
maybe we have to go to a beach?"

"Oooh, Glitter Beach!" gasped Jasmine,
pointing to a label. "Somewhere with a name
like that is bound to have sparkling sand."

Ellie and Summer nodded eagerly. Jasmine's
hazel eyes shone in excitement. "What are we
waiting for? Let's call Trixi!"

The girls put their hands on the green gems
of the box. "The answer to the riddle is Glitter
Beach!" they said together.

There was a bright flash of light and a
familiar little pixie hovered in front of them on a
floating leaf!

"Trixibelle!" cried Jasmine happily. "You've

come to take us on another
adventure!"

"Hello, girls!" Trixi smiled.

"You look pretty!" Ellie
said. Trixi was wearing a
bright yellow dress made
out of sunflower petals
and a garland of
multicoloured flowers
hung around her neck.

"I was just getting ready
to go on holiday with my fairy friend, Willow,"
Trixi said with a big smile. "All the fairies in
the kingdom meet up every Midsummer's Eve
at Glitter Beach to watch the kingdom's magic
being renewed!"

"Oh!" Ellie exclaimed. "The riddle said
something about midsummer and Glitter
Beach."

Trixi's blue eyes widened. "Oh no! Perhaps Queen Malice's horrible thunderbolt is going to ruin the special fairy day!"

"Don't worry," Ellie said. "We'll come with you to Glitter Beach. If a thunderbolt has landed there, we'll fix things!"

"Oh, thank you!" Trixi said gratefully. She tapped her magic ring and chanted:

"The evil queen has trouble planned.
Brave helpers fly to save our land!"

As she spoke, the girls were surrounded by shards of sunlight. Round and round they whirled until the magic set them down gently. There was the feel of sunshine on their skin and a gentle rocking under their feet.

"Wow!" Ellie breathed as she opened her eyes. They were standing in a boat made out of a

large white shell, which was being pulled by two huge silver dolphins. They were heading towards a small harbour with a shimmering beach.

"We're tiny!" Ellie realised suddenly as she saw that she was the same height as Trixi.

'That's why the dolphins look so big!" exclaimed Summer.

"I thought I'd make you small so you can enjoy Glitter Beach properly. There's lots to see

and do but it's all
built for fairies!"
Trixi explained.

"It's just
amazing being
this small,"
said Summer,
throwing her
arms around
Trixi. "It's lovely to
be able to hug you!"

Ellie put her hand to
the top of her head to check for the tiara that
always appeared when she went to the Secret
Kingdom. Sure enough, it was there, reduced
to teeny-tiny size just as Ellie was. Jasmine and
Summer were wearing theirs too. The tiaras
showed that the girls were Very Important
Friends of King Merry!

"Glitter Beach is just ahead." Trixi waved an arm towards the harbour. The girls could just see pretty little shops and market stalls in the bay, and multicoloured boats tied to the pier.

"Look, the boats have got wings instead of sails!" Jasmine called out as they got closer.

Trixi managed to smile. "That's because those are fairy yachts. They fly as well as sail!"

All around them, fairies
were surfing on
long, flat, mussel
shells. They
raced across
the waves,
their wings
shimmering
in the
sunlight. One
was even doing
a handstand on his

board. He came zooming past the girls.

"Amazing!" said Jasmine.

"Glitter Beach is one of the most important
places in the whole kingdom," Trixi said. "At
twelve o'clock every Midsummer's Eve the
golden sand turns to glitter dust for one minute.
In that time all the magic is returned to the

land for another year. The fairies always come to watch, but I've never seen it before – I can't wait! Without the sand at Glitter Beach there would be no magic anywhere in the kingdom."

"Oh, wow!" breathed Ellie.

"We can't forget about Queen Malice's thunderbolt," Summer warned. "We have to find it before it causes trouble."

Ellie and Jasmine nodded.

The dolphins pulled up to the wooden pier and the girls climbed out of the shell boat.

As Trixi flew her leaf out of the boat another fairy rushed over and hugged her. Her delicate wings were as aquamarine as the sea, and she had wild flowers in her hair.

"Hello!" she said delightedly.

"Ellie, Summer and Jasmine, this is my fairy friend, Willow," Trixi introduced them.

Willow stared at their tiaras. "You must be

the human girls who've been finding Queen
Malice's thunderbolts," she exclaimed, her wings
fluttering. "I'm so glad to meet you!"

Trixi gave a sad smile. "We think there's a
thunderbolt here at Glitter Beach."

"Oh no!" Willow gasped.

"We have to find it before it ruins the
ceremony," Ellie added. "Will you help us look?"

Willow flew off to the harbour and the girls and Trixi looked all around the pretty little shops and stalls, but they couldn't spot anything suspicious.

Just then Ellie caught sight of a dark cloud heading across the water towards Glitter Beach. It was shaped like a funnel and was swirling round and round. There were cries of alarm as the fairies noticed it too.

"Quick! It's a whirlwind! Get inside!" The shouts rang out.

The girls and Trixi hid in a tiny shop with lots of other fairies.

"Look!" Summer cried as the whirlwind reached the beach. All the beautiful golden sand started to swirl up from the ground into it. "It's taking all the sand!"

The fairies shouted, trying to cast spells to stop it – but nothing worked.

Just then Jasmine caught sight of figures moving in the swirling smoke. "Storm Sprites!" she cried, pointing at the shadowy shapes.

The sprites screeched with laughter as the

tornado whipped around. Soon the sand was gone, and the girls could see that the wind was coming from a jagged shape in the ground.

"It's the thunderbolt!" Summer breathed. It was buried deep in the earth, with just its black tip showing.

"It was buried under the sand!" Ellie gasped.

The tornado swept away and everyone stared in disbelief. Every single grain of beautiful, sparkling sand had disappeared!

All that was left of the beach was dull rock. "This is awful!" Trixi cried. "It's getting dark now, and if the sand's not here when the clock strikes twelve, there'll be no magic in the kingdom for a whole year!"

"Don't worry," Ellie said, putting her arm around Trixi. "We'll break the thunderbolt and get the sand back before midnight."

Jasmine nodded. "We've defeated Queen Malice before and we can do it again!"

Trixi sighed. "I'd better ask King Merry to come. He'll need to know what his rotten sister has been up to." Trixi tapped her ring and King Merry's name appeared in silvery letters in the air. "He'll come as soon as he gets the message," Trixi continued. "He's at the Enchanted Palace, so he can use the rainbow slide in the garden pond to get anywhere in the kingdom."

"In the meantime we'd better start thinking of how we can sort this out!" said Jasmine determinedly.

The girls walked around the rocky beach, comforting all the fairies they met.

Suddenly, they spotted something in the sea.

"It's King Merry – and he's on water-skis!" gasped Jasmine.

The little round king headed towards them. Two dolphins were towing him through the waves! He was wearing long, brightly patterned shorts and yellow armbands. His crown was perched on top of a white sun hat.

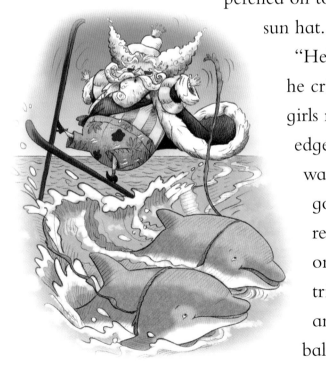

"Hello, hello!" he cried as the girls ran to the edge of the water. Letting go of the reins with one hand, he tried to wave and lost his balance.

"Oh dear!" Trixi's hand flew to her mouth as the king toppled backwards into the water. "Back in a minute!" Trixi cried as she zoomed over to him on her leaf.

The girls saw her tapping her pixie ring. The king rose from the water and began to drift magically across the top of the waves.

Trixi's magic put him gently down on the beach, and Ellie, Summer and Jasmine rushed over to him. The girls suddenly felt very small so Trixi turned the three friends back to their normal size.

"I came as fast as I could," said the king anxiously. "What has my sister done now?"

"Her thunderbolt has stolen all the sand from Glitter Beach," Trixi cried. "There's not a single grain left, Your Majesty!"

"A tornado came and whisked the sand away so fast," said Jasmine.

"Yes," Ellie added thoughtfully. "But where did the tornado take the sand?"

"Maybe one of the fairies noticed," said Jasmine. "Let's ask around."

Summer, Ellie and Jasmine started asking the fairies about the tornado, but no one had seen where it went.

"It's no good," said Summer, sitting down on the rocky beach. The cloud of fairies fluttered overhead. Ellie and Jasmine sat down too, and then Ellie noticed a familiar-looking fairy flitting nearby. She looked closely and realised it was Willow. She looked so tiny now!

"Hello," Ellie smiled and put out her hand. The little fairy landed on it, light as a feather on her palm.

Willow looked at them with wide eyes. "I saw where the tornado went! I watched it swirl into that cave over there," she said, pointing to where there were some steep grey cliffs jutting out into

the bay. The girls could just see a cave at the
base of the cliffs.

"Brilliant!" said Jasmine. "Well done, Willow!"
The little fairy beamed proudly.

The girls hurried across the beach.

"Look!" Jasmine hissed as they got closer to
the cave. She pointed ahead. Even though it was
quite dark, they could just make out lots of little
footprints in the mud around its entrance.

"It must be the Storm Sprites!" A shiver ran down Ellie's spine as she thought about Queen Malice's spiky-haired servants.

"What are they doing in the cave?" Summer asked shakily.

Jasmine squared her shoulders and looked at them both. "There's only one way to find out. Come on!"

Jasmine, Summer and Ellie tiptoed up to the cave entrance. They could hear the Storm

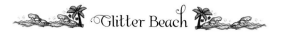

Sprites shouting at one another.

"Hurry up!" one of them yelled. "Once Queen Malice has this sand no one will be able to get in her way any more!"

The girls crept forwards and peered into the dark cave. Inside was a mountain of glittering golden sand. Eight Storm Sprites were shovelling it into sacks.

"The sprites are going to take the sand to Queen Malice!" said Jasmine. "We've got to stop them!"

"Yoo hoo! Girls!" a voice called, making them jump.

King Merry was waving
as he climbed clumsily
over the rocks. Trixi
was hovering behind
him, holding his
cloak up in the air.

"Shhh!' Jasmine
hissed, rushing over to
where the king was.

"We need to find
a way to get the sand
back," said Summer.

Ellie frowned thoughtfully.
"Maybe we can sneak in and take the sacks?"

"But the Storm Sprites will see us," Jasmine
pointed out.

"The pearl!" Summer exclaimed. "The
mermaids gave us a pearl that we could use to
turn ourselves invisible!"

There was a bright silver flash and Jasmine gasped as the Magic Box appeared in her arms!

The lid of the box slowly started to open. Tucked inside one of the little wooden compartments lay a glowing, shimmering silver pearl.

Summer took the pearl out of the box. Almost immediately her fingers and hands vanished and then she disappeared completely!

"Here, hold my hand!" Summer's voice came from behind them.

Jasmine felt Summer's hand touch hers. She grabbed Ellie's fingers with her other hand. Holding on to one another, all three girls were completely invisible!

"Good luck!" Trixi and the king called as the girls set off to the cave. It was very dark inside. Ellie, Summer and Jasmine held their breath as they tiptoed further into the cave.

Clunk!

Ellie tripped over a shovel lying on the ground and it banged against the rocks. The sprites looked up. The girls froze. A horrible thought crossed Jasmine's mind – the pearl would only keep them invisible for a short while!

"What was that noise?" asked one sprite.

"I don't know," said another. They looked around suspiciously.

The girls stayed as still as they could. Summer was sure the sprites must be able to hear her heart hammering in her chest.

The sprites slowly got back to work. Jasmine continued to lead the way to the back of the cave but as she did so, she felt a sneeze building in her nose. She swallowed, trying to hold it in, but it was no good…all of a sudden it burst out!

"Ahh-chooo!"

All the sprites jumped.

"Who's there?" one of them called.

"Maybe…maybe it's a ghost," said the smallest sprite.

"Don't be a nincompoop," another sprite told him. "There's no such thing as ghosts."

But Ellie saw that all the sprites had started to look worried. *That's it!* she thought. She tugged on Jasmine's hand and whispered as quietly as she could.

"If we pretend to be ghosts we'll scare them so much that they'll run away!"

Jasmine passed the message on to Summer and then kicked over a nearby sack.

The sprites jumped back in alarm as it fell.

Jasmine took a deep breath and started to make a strange howling, moaning noise.

"Argh!" the sprites all yelled. The smallest sprite backed up so quickly he tripped over his spade and fell to the ground, sending the sprite next to him sprawling. Ellie and Summer joined

in with ghostly noises. Jasmine was very good
at acting and she put on her best spooky voice.
"We're the ghosts of Glitter Caves and we're
coming to get youuuuuuuuu!"

The sprites started to yell and run around. As
one ran near them, Ellie had an idea. Using her
free hand, she reached out and tickled the sprite.

"Argh! Eee!" he yelled. "The ghost's got me!"

Ellie had to fight back her giggles. "I am the
Tickle Monster Ghost!" she said in a spooky
voice like Jasmine. "Beware! Bewaaaaaaaaare!"

She poked and
prodded the
sprites while
Jasmine made
spooky noises
and Summer
pushed the
sacks over.

"Forget the silly magic sand!" the smallest sprite shouted. "I'm getting out of here!"

"Me too!" yelled another.

All the sprites ran out of the cave and onto the rocky beach. They flapped over the water, splashing and yelling about ghosts.

"We did it!" Summer said.

"And only just in time!" said Jasmine as they

all slowly shimmered into view again.

"And now we can get the sand back to the beach!" said Ellie.

"Noooooo!" A screech of rage rang through the cave. The girls jumped and swung around. There, standing right in the entrance of the cave, was Queen Malice herself!

The wicked queen's midnight-dark eyes flashed with fury.

She pointed at the girls with a bony finger. "How dare you keep coming to this land to stop my magic? You will not break my sixth thunderbolt!"

"Malice!" King Merry's voice rang out as he hurried to the cave entrance. "Please stop behaving like this."

"Who are you to tell me what to do?" hissed Queen Malice.

"He's the king!" said Trixi with a very cross

look on her face.

The queen glared.
"Ha! I won't listen
to him or you!"
She flicked her
fingers and a mini
thunderbolt flew
from them.

Trixi tried to dodge out of the way, but the
thunderbolt caught her leaf and
she was thrown through the air.

Luckily Trixi landed in a
heap of sand. She pointed
her ring at the queen
defiantly, but only a
few sparks appeared.
"Oh no," Trixi cried
unhappily. "My
magic is all gone!"

Queen Malice screeched with laughter.
"After today no one in the kingdom will have
any magic – I'll have it all!" Her voice rose in
triumph. "And it will make me more powerful
than ever!"

With a clap of her hands, she vanished –
taking all the sand with her!

Ellie, Jasmine and Summer stared in horror.

"Now what are we going to
do?" exclaimed Jasmine.

With the pile of sand
gone, Trixi was left
sitting on the cave
floor. She burst
into tears.

King Merry
pointed outside.
Night had fallen
while they had

been in the cave, and the beach was bathed in moonlight. "We're running out of time."

"There must be a way to fix things," said Jasmine, pacing up and down.

"Usually, to break the thunderbolt, we need to reverse the magic," Summer said thoughtfully. "This thunderbolt has stolen the sand. If we can put it back on the beach, then maybe the spell will be broken."

"But we don't have any sand," Ellie pointed out. "Queen Malice has taken it all."

"Not all of it!" Summer gasped. "Look!" She pointed at Trixi. She was covered with fine grains of shimmering sand from when she had been knocked into the pile by Queen Malice. "We just have to take the sand to the beach!"

Summer had just stepped out of the cave, carrying Trixi carefully in her hands, when a bony leg tripped her over!

Trixi managed to jump on her leaf before she crashed to the ground, but as she did so a few of the tiny grains of sand on her clothes fell off. "The sand!" she cried.

An evil laugh came from behind her. A Storm Sprite was flapping towards her.

More and more Storm Sprites appeared and tried to grab Trixi. She managed to dive out of their reach, but sand kept falling from her.

"We have to try and catch the sand," Ellie

told Summer. The girls ran underneath Trixi as she zoomed around, holding their hands up to catch the falling grains. King Merry held his cloak out and tried to catch some too.

Just then a cloud of furious fairies arrived!

"Go away, you horrid sprites!" one shouted.

"How dare you steal our sand!" cried another.

The fairies flew all around the Storm Sprites, keeping just out of reach of their pointy fingers. There were so many fairies that the sprites couldn't see if Trixi was among them.

"Psst!" came a tiny voice from below them. "I'm down here!" Trixi was on the ground, hiding behind a rock.

The girls and King Merry crept over to her. The little pixie looked very sad. "I lost the sand," she cried. Her shoulders dropped. She turned to look at the beach. "The sand is supposed to be so beautiful, glinting in the moonlight," she said

sadly. "I wish we could have seen it."

"I can!" Summer gasped. She pointed at King Merry's purple cloak. There, twinkling like a golden star, was a single grain of sand!

"Hold still, King Merry," Jasmine said,

carefully reaching towards the precious grain of sand. "Quickly! We have to put it on the beach before the clock strikes midnight!"

Running as fast as they could, the girls rushed to the beach.

"Here goes!" cried Jasmine, delicately placing the glimmering grain onto the rocky shore.

The friends held hands as the sand touched the grey rocks. For a second, nothing happened. Then, with a massive crack, the thunderbolt on the beach shattered into black fragments!

Ellie felt something falling on her. It felt like the finest, lightest rain. Looking up, she gasped. "It's raining sand!"

The sand floated down from the sky, shining in the moonlight and tickling the girls' skin.

"It worked!" cried Trixi as the fairies started to dance and fly in the glittering air.

"We did it," gasped Ellie, hugging the others.

"We've broken the spell and the sand's back!"

King Merry threw his crown into the air in joy. "We've saved the day – I mean, the night – and we've destroyed my sister's last thunderbolt!" He began to dance a jig.

Jasmine grabbed the others' hands and pulled them around in a circle. The sand felt soft beneath their feet and they swirled faster and faster, shrieking in delight.

All around them fairies fluttered excitedly, laughing and shouting for joy.

Trixi swooped down to the girls. "It's nearly midnight!" she cried excitedly. "The midsummer magic is about to start!"

The sand on the beach began to sparkle and glow as if it were made of lots of tiny jewels. The glow flooded over King Merry, Trixi, and the girls, too, making their skin tingle and buzz.

"Glitter dust," King Merry said with a sigh of

contentment. "The magic is working!"

"Look how happy everyone is," murmured Ellie as two fairies fluttered past, looping in the air as the clock rang out twelve times.

On the final chime, there was a bright silver flash and then the sparkling sand became a soft shimmering gold again.

"We've all got our magic back for another year, thanks to you," Trixi cried. "Look!" She pointed in front of her. "Shining star!" she declared. A star appeared and floated

towards the pixie.

"You didn't use your ring! Does that mean we could do magic too?" Ellie asked curiously.

"Perhaps," Trixi laughed. "Why don't you try?"

Summer thought for a moment. "Um, a flower!" she said. There was a bright flash and a golden flower appeared!

Ellie couldn't resist. "I'd like a drawing set!" A sketchbook appeared, along with a box containing pencils in every possible colour!

"My turn!" said Jasmine excitedly. "I'd love a guitar," she called. A guitar appeared at once with strings made of shining gold. Jasmine remembered the song she had once played for the king's birthday and began to play it again now, changing a few lines:

"The Secret Kingdom is a magical place,
Even the moon has a smiley face.
Midsummer's Eve is a time of fun,
Now that Malice's meanness is quite
undone."

When the song ended, King Merry walked
over to the water's edge and called for silence.

"Thanks to our human friends, all six
thunderbolts have been found and the danger to
our wonderful kingdom has passed."

A worrying thought crossed Ellie's mind. Now
that the thunderbolts had been found, would she,
Summer and Jasmine be needed in the Secret
Kingdom again?

The king continued talking. "To say thank
you, I have a gift for you three." He handed the

girls a bag made of glittering silver material.

"There is glitter dust in this bag," the king explained. "If you need to, you can use it to cast a spell. But use it wisely. There is only enough for one spell each."

It was an amazing present, but Jasmine felt like she was about to cry. Did this mean they wouldn't have any more magical adventures?

"King Merry, is this the last time we'll visit the Secret Kingdom?" Jasmine burst out.

Just then there was a noise from the sea and a small black boat came flying over the waves.

"It's Queen Malice!" gasped Trixi.

Two fierce sea serpents pulled the queen's black boat. It stopped near the shore. "You think you've defeated me," the wicked queen cried, "but I'll be back! Here's a little something for you to remember me by!" She clapped her hands and a thunderbolt shot towards the beach!

"How can we stop it?" cried Summer.

"Tonight our magic is extra strong!" Trixi shouted. "If we all work together, we

can break the thunderbolt!"

She pointed her hands at the thunderbolt
and every fairy did the same. Ellie, Jasmine and
Summer copied. Suddenly, silvery blue light shot
out from their hands.

The thunderbolt hit the blue light and
shattered into a million pieces, which flew
towards Queen Malice.

"Nooooooo!" she screeched, diving into the
water as the shards hit her boat. The Storm
Sprites climbed onto one of the sea serpents and
helped a soggy Queen Malice onto another.
"You haven't seen the last of me!" she shouted as
the serpent carried her away.

"You asked me whether you will come back,"
King Merry said softly. "Well, I have a feeling
that we will need your help again very soon."

Ellie, Jasmine and Summer looked at one
another and smiled.

"We'll come whenever you need us," Ellie promised.

"And we'll fight whatever Queen Malice throws at us!" Jasmine said.

King Merry clapped. "The time has come to say farewell – for now." He turned to the girls. "Thank you, from the bottom of all our hearts."

Trixi flew over to them, tears in her blue eyes. "I'll miss all of you so much!"

"We'll miss you too," Ellie told her, feeling her own eyes prickle.

The girls waved to all their magical friends, then joined hands. Trixi tapped her ring and a

sparkly whirlwind swirled around them. They were scooped up into the air and whisked away.

They landed safely back in Ellie's bedroom. For a moment, they all blinked.

"We're home," Ellie said softly.

"The box too," said Summer in relief, looking down at the Magic Box, which was sitting safely on the rug in front of them.

The lid opened and the girls placed their precious bag of glitter dust inside.

"We've had some amazing adventures," said Jasmine as the box slowly shut.

"We will go back, won't we?" Summer asked.

"Yes, we'll go back and have new adventures," Ellie said, feeling certain.

The friends smiled at one another. The Secret Kingdom was waiting for them. One day the Magic Box would glow again – and they could hardly wait!

Goodbye!

Thanks for joining Ellie, Jasmine and Summer on their adventures through the Secret Kingdom. We couldn't have found all those thunderbolts without you!

I hope that you've enjoyed reading these stories and that you'll come back to visit us in the Secret Kingdom. Something tells me we haven't seen the last of Queen Malice and her Storm Sprites, so we're sure to need your help again...

See you soon!

Love and kisses,

Trixi
x x x

Secret Kingdom

Collect them all!

Series One

Enchanted Palace
ROSIE BANKS

Unicorn Valley
ROSIE BANKS

Cloud Island
ROSIE BANKS

Magic Mountain
ROSIE BANKS

Mermaid Reef
ROSIE BANKS

Glitter Beach
ROSIE BANKS

Series Two

Bubble Volcano
ROSIE BANKS

Starspout Bakery
ROSIE BANKS

Dream Dale
ROSIE BANKS

Lily Pad Lake
ROSIE BANKS

Fairytale Forest
ROSIE BANKS

Untangled Glade
ROSIE BANKS

Series Three

Wildflower Wood
ROSIE BANKS

Swan Palace
ROSIE BANKS

Snow Bear Sanctuary
ROSIE BANKS

Phoenix Festival
ROSIE BANKS

Fancy Dress Party
ROSIE BANKS

Jewel Cavern
ROSIE BANKS

Series Four

Series Five

Secret Kingdom — Puppy Fun — ROSIE BANKS

Secret Kingdom — Magic Seal — ROSIE BANKS

Secret Kingdom — Emerald Unicorn — ROSIE BANKS

Secret Kingdom — Sapphire Spell — ROSIE BANKS

Secret Kingdom — Glitter Bird — ROSIE BANKS

Secret Kingdom — Rainbow Lion — ROSIE BANKS

Secret Kingdom — Diamond Wings — ROSIE BANKS

Secret Kingdom — Ruby Riddle — ROSIE BANKS

5 amazing bumper specials!

Secret Kingdom — Christmas Castle — ROSIE BANKS

Secret Kingdom — Dolphin Bay — ROSIE BANKS

Secret Kingdom — Christmas Ballerina — ROSIE BANKS

Secret Kingdom — Pixie Princess — ROSIE BANKS

Secret Kingdom — Starlight Adventure — ROSIE BANKS

Have you read all the
Secret Kingdom
adventures?

Secret Kingdom

A magical world of
friendship and fun!

Join the Secret Kingdom Club at

www.secretkingdombooks.com

and enjoy games, sneak peeks and lots more!

You'll find great activities, competitions, stories
and games, plus a special newsletter for
Secret Kingdom friends!